"I'm a great admirer of Mickey Friedman's work. Elegant, vivid, and confident, THE FAULT TREE transcends the 'mystery' genre but is wonderfully mysterious."

Diane Johnson

"FULL OF DANGER AND BREATHLESS ACTION . . .

Very skillfully plotted. There are well-laid clues to reward the reader who is not swept away. Another cornerstone of Friedman's writing is carefully researched and vividly drawn settings. Her Indian cities and countrysides are as convincing as the Florida coast in HURRICANE SEASON."

San Jose Mercury News

"She has a knack for adventure scenes, and the fearfulness of a couple of encounters is sweaty-palm real. Her most impressive quality, though, is her way of using recognizable emotion, in this case the guilt most of us endure regarding some sibling, to force her readers to identify with the people on the page."

St. Petersburg Times

"Friedman cleverly weaves the threads of past and present into a cogent tale that speeds the reader through mystic India and home again in an adventure that both thrills and logically unveils an elusive mystery."

Library Journal

Also by Mickey Friedman
*Published by Ballantine Books*:

HURRICANE SEASON

# THE FAULT TREE

## Mickey Friedman

BALLANTINE BOOKS • NEW YORK

Copyright © 1984 by Mickey Friedman

Library of Congress Catalog Card Number: 84-13741

ISBN 0-345-32198-7

This edition published by arrangement with E. P. Dutton, Inc.

**Printed in Canada**

First Ballantine Books Edition: September 1985

TO MY MOTHER

# Acknowledgments

Ernie Eason patiently and imaginatively contributed his technical expertise to this book. I couldn't have done it without him, and am deeply grateful. Thanks are due to Kirin Contractor for her invaluable advice and to David Mandelbaum, who answered some of my questions about India.

Responsibility for the many liberties taken with their areas of expertise is mine.

I would also like to thank Steve Whealton, Alan Friedman and Paul De Angelis for their help.

Some details of Indian serpent-worship were taken from *Indian Serpent-Lore: Or, the Nagas in Hindu Legend and Art* by J. Ph. Vogel (Arthur Probsthain, London, 1926).

I am grateful to Dr. G. Nagarajan, of Bangalore, India, who I hope will not regret telling me the meaning of his name.

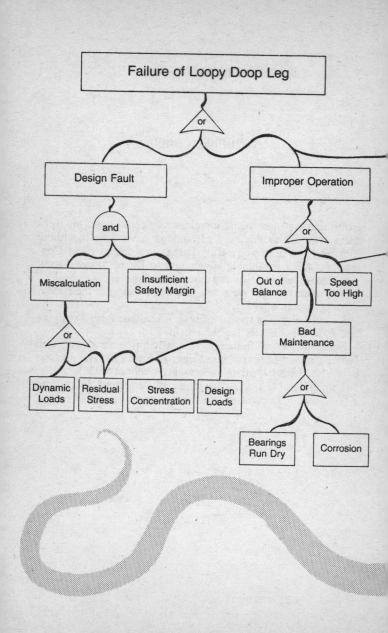

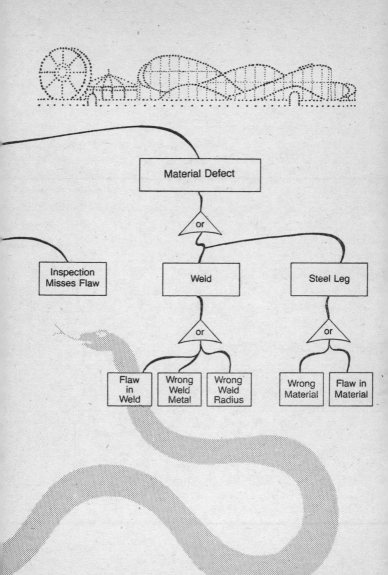

# India

## The Mid-1970s

MARINA'S KNEES JERKED AND SHE AWAKENED from a dream of falling. The chant in her head dissolved into the chatter of her fellow passengers. A damp spot on the greasy window of the bus showed where her forehead had touched it. She tried to swallow a bitter taste.

The chant was lurking, waiting to start up again, caught in her brain like an advertising jingle. *Guru Nagarajan, Parama Sukhadam. Guru Nagarajan, Chrana Shranam.* After Nagarajan had been taken away she had listened to them all night, Catherine and the other two, their voices wavering, trailing off, then coming back louder and stronger. Exiled as she had been from the first, she sat alone on her bed mat, then later moved out to the veranda.

Palika Road wasn't sleeping either. Shadowy figures moved along it; lights flickered in the mud-colored houses that were hardly more than huts. Wails from the house of the More family made the hair on her arms stand up.

At first light the chanting had stopped and the three of them appeared on the veranda—Catherine, Joe, who was a spindly boy with acne, and plain, round-faced Denise in her wire-rimmed glasses. They looked gray in the gray light, and she could hardly see their faces. They ignored her, brushing past her to descend the steps, until she cleared her throat and said, "Where are you going?"

Catherine hesitated, then turned toward her with the reluctance Marina had come to expect. "To the jail. To see Nagarajan." Her voice, hoarse from chanting, was almost a whisper.

At one time, Marina would have said the things that came into her mind: that the police were unlikely to let Nagarajan's followers visit him, that walking down Palika Road might be dangerous under the circumstances, that the best thing would be to wait. Now, she said, "OK."

Catherine started toward the others, then returned to Marina. She reached out and took Marina's wrist, and Marina's knees gave slightly. Marina looked down at the cheap bangles on Catherine's thin arm, the ring with a pink stone on her middle finger. She didn't want to look at Catherine's face, but when Catherine didn't let go Marina's eyes moved upward. Catherine's hair, the hair Nagarajan admired so much, hung greasy and limp. Shadowed by the edge of her sari, her face seemed sunken. "You're happy now. This is what you wanted," Catherine croaked.

Marina wondered if Catherine could feel the tremor that moved through her body. It came, not from fear, but from a weird exultation that Catherine had, voluntarily, touched her, spoken to her.

She wet her lips, trying to choose a response, but Catherine let go and turned away. Marina watched them cross the strip of packed earth to the gate, then go down the road in the growing light. They had not returned when, in the blazing midmorning, Marina splashed her body with tepid water, put on fresh clothes, and went to catch the bus for Bombay.

*Guru Nagarajan, Parama Sukhadam. Guru Nagarajan, Chrana Shranam.* Guru Nagarajan, Eternal giver of happiness. Guru Nagarajan, We take refuge at his feet. The damp spot her forehead had made was dry now, another smudge on a window covered with smudges. Through it, she watched the outskirts of Halapur come into view and slide past as they neared the center of town. Bullocks nosed the earth in the blasted garden of the District Administration Center. Posters of men with guns chasing other men with guns were plastered outside the Town Talkies movie theater. An old man laboriously pedaled a bicycle whose rear baskets were full of empty milk bottles.

The staff at the consulate in Bombay was accustomed to seeing Marina, and usually paid little attention to her. Today it had been different, because of Nagarajan's arrest. She was allowed to see someone right away. The plastic nameplate beside the door said "M. Hayes."

"A situation like this brings out strong feelings," Mr. Hayes said. "The Indian people don't understand these Westerners claiming to be practicing some form of Hinduism, and many of them don't particularly like it." Despite the heat, his tie was knotted tightly at the neck of his white short-sleeved shirt. The blinds were drawn

3

against the glare, and the breeze from the ceiling fan stirred the papers on his desk and Marina's damp hair. If only she could bend and rest her head on the arm of her chair she could sleep.

"Strong feelings," Mr. Hayes said. "We'll send someone this afternoon. How many did you say are living there?"

She roused herself to answer. "People come and go all the time, but right now there are my sister and me and two other Americans. An Indian man named Joginder looks after the place, but he doesn't live there. Compared with some of the other sects, it's very small."

"I suppose this Nagarajan is claiming he didn't kill the boy?"

"I don't know. Nobody at the ashram has told me anything. They went this morning to try to see him, but they hadn't gotten back when I left."

Perspiration had made yellow stains under the arms of Mr. Hayes's shirt. "I wish to God these kids would all stay home," he said.

The bus pulled up at Halapur's central square, causing its usual flurry of quickly extinguished interest in the passersby. As always, a knot of men squatted under the peepul tree chewing betel, and women lingered at the public pump, balancing babies or clay jars on their hips, while birds fluttered in the spilled water curling over the muddy stones. When Marina stepped out of the bus, the sun hit her face like a slap. She started back through town to the ashram.

Black birds wheeled against the hot blue sky. A bullock cart rattled past her, raising dust that settled in her throat. When she reached Palika Road, she heard a roaring sound that suggested nothing. The sound had been in her ears several minutes before it occurred to her that it might be voices, and she saw the mass of people far down toward the ashram. As she continued walking, shading her eyes, a figure detached itself and ran toward her. It was Joginder, his turban disarranged, his eyes bloodshot. "Come away, miss!" he cried, and when she stood, confused, he gestured violently. Something in his movement animated her, and she followed him down a side street, stumbling, infected by his terror.

They passed a bicycle repair shed, its dirt yard filled with bicycles swaying against one another, and went through a gate into an earthen courtyard. Three string cots almost filled the small space, and bedraggled chickens scratched and pecked in the shade of a dusty, broad-leafed tree. Joginder sank down on one of the cots, trembling, and she said, "Joginder, what's happening?"

"It is burning," he said, and at that instant she smelled smoke.

# California

## The Mid-1980s

### RISK

Things you should know about risk:
1. Risk is always present. There is no such thing as zero risk.
2. Actual risk may differ greatly from perceived risk.
3. If you reduce risk, you may reduce benefits.
4. You must decide what level of risk is acceptable for your situation.

Excerpt from *Why Breakdown?*
—company brochure for Breakdown, Inc.

THE FUN WORLD MAINTENANCE CHIEF breathed heavily, emphysemically. "—inspected daily," he was saying. "Nothing like this ever happened—"

But now it has, Marina thought, and what that means

is just dawning on you. The sky was dark now, the wind steady and cold. The ambulances had left, but the television people were still around, preparing their stories for the eleven o'clock news.

The maintenance chief looked about sixty. His face was yellow in the glare of the lights. When talk about blame started—and it had started already, she imagined, on the news bulletins—the maintenance crew would be the first to go up against the wall. There would be portentous discussions about "human error," as if most things didn't go wrong because a human made a mistake at one point or another. "Every day," the chief said. His words had a phlegmy roughness. "Mr. Bolton insists."

It took Marina a moment or two to put together "Mr. Bolton" and Bobo the Clown. "Why would it break?" the chief said, and began to gargle and wheeze.

Marina looked past the maintenance chief's pinkening ear. It was time for a cup of coffee. She disliked these scenes—the self-justification, the assertions of blame-lessness, the constant terror of being found in the wrong. People never realized that charm, self-pity, excuses couldn't change what the numbers told her and were a waste of her time. She'd look at the records and make the measurements and if the maintenance chief had done his job right he'd be OK. Meanwhile—"Excuse me," she said, and walked away.

She went to pick up her kit, one of the leather cases she and her colleagues, with heavy irony, called their "doctor's bags"—and stopped to listen to a wispy teenaged girl talking to a television crew. A drop of blood had dried under one of the girl's nostrils. "They were having a good time," the girl said. "Laughing and all. They rode twice."

7

A woman in a blazer checked a clipboard. "You're taking about Randy and Annette Wilson?"

"The fat ones."

The girl looked shocked, but excited too, and gratified at the attention she was getting. Marina had seen it dozens of times. First you had to coax and cajole the story out of them and then, about the time you had all you needed, they started to like it and wouldn't leave you alone.

She wiped her hands on the front of the jumpsuit she wore over her jeans, picked up her bag, and took another look at Loopy Doop.

It was beautiful. Magnificent, really, with its long, spiderlike legs ending in bright pink-and-yellow gondolas. A lovely, elegant design. What a shame that an hour or so ago one of those attenuated steel legs had given way and sent the gondola carrying Randy and Annette Wilson, who liked Loopy Doop enough to ride it twice in a row, smashing into the ticket booth.

She had taken a close look as soon as she arrived, while they were still loading Randy and Annette and the ticket-taker and the kid and his mother who'd been buying tickets into ambulances and hoping they might make it to the hospital. The leg had broken right next to the hub. She had eyeballed the fracture, photographed it, and made an impression of the surface with dental imprint material. She could tell by looking that it was a fatigue failure caused by the steel tubing bending back and forth. What had caused it to bend was another question.

She'd have to get someone to come out with a saw to cut the fracture surface out and take it back to the lab so she could study it and have specimens made up for tests.

A shame. It had been beautiful.

She picked her way through the shards of glass around the wrecked ticket booth and went to look for coffee.


Marina got out her notebook and started a list.

She had: taken the photos, made a sketch of the scene, gotten names and phone numbers of witnesses, examined and made an imprint of the break. She needed to: get the Loopy Doop specifications from somebody, the inspection records from somebody—she'd ask the maintenance chief, if he'd gotten his breath back—get the piece of Loopy Doop's leg sawed off.

She sipped watery coffee from a Styrofoam cup. In the background, a radio murmured about "the Loopy Doop disaster." She was sitting in the Bobobar, a juice bar that had been left open when the park was closed after the accident. A bigger-than-life-sized Bobo the Clown was stenciled on the wall in red.

It was chance that she'd been at the office and the maintenance chief had gotten her instead of the service. This was going to be a big case—exactly the macabre kind of scenario the press adored, which meant Sandy would probably take it himself. So what if she'd been here first and done the groundwork.

The smell of stale beer and cigarette smoke wafted over her, and she looked up to see a man with thinning hair and a medium-sized paunch, a cup of coffee in one hand and a cigarette in the other. He sank into the chair across from her and nodded at her notebook. "Who're you covering it for?"

"I'm not a reporter."

"Police?" The man put his cup down and pulled a ball-point pen and a thin tan-colored notebook, spiral-bound at the top, out of the inside pocket of his corduroy jacket.

"No."

"Then what—oh, right." He pointed at the red-stitched "Breakdown, Inc." on the pocket of her jumpsuit. "The disastermongers. Down on the water-front. You on the job here?"

"I can't say anything right now."

The man clicked his pen. "You're here, right? Looks to me like you're working. Who're you working for? Bobo? Get him off the hook?"

If she got into the papers without Sandy's OK it would be a major misstep. "I can't say anything."

The man scribbled something. "Sure. What's your name?"

"I said I can't—"

"OK, OK. Who called you in?"

The tightness was starting in her forehead. It was the same tightness she sometimes felt when, as an expert witness, she was being cross-examined by a hostile attorney. "I absolutely am not going to say anything. I have to get on with what I'm doing, so—"

The man shrugged and closed his notebook. His mouth twisted in a sour little smile. "Grist for the mill to you people, I guess. It's an ill wind that doesn't blow somebody some good, right?"

Marina watched him wander off. Ill Winds, Inc. She had a Ph.D. in engineering. She could have been building bridges. In her mind, she saw buzzards, their wingspans huge, wheeling in a blazing blue sky. This kind of work was perfect for her. She bent back to her list.

A navy-blue Porsche with BRKDWN license plates was pulled up near the ticket booth. Sandy must have gotten the message she'd left with the service. She looked around and saw him in the shadow of Loopy Doop talking to the maintenance chief. The jeans, deck shoes, and fisherman's sweater he was wearing meant he'd spent the afternoon on his sailboat, the *Disaster-Pro*.

Now, Marina would be relegated to supporting player. When Sandy was in a scene, he was the lead. He beckoned her over. With his lean body, his tan, his gray hair ruffling in the wind, he so outshone the maintenance chief that the other man might not have been there at all.

"Marina, I think you've already met Ed, here. I was just telling him how fortunate it is that he called us in so soon after the accident." Sandy's voice was somber, but managed to convey congratulations to Ed for his good sense.

"I didn't even wait to get authorization," Ed said. From his tone Marina guessed he was as dazed by that fact as by the tragedy itself.

"It makes all the difference in the world when we can get on the scene fast," Sandy said.

What's this *we*? It was good old Marina who was working on a Sunday afternoon and jumped into her Toyota to drive down to Redwood City and take care of business. *I* wasn't out of touch on some boat with a cutesy name getting myself written up in the society columns.

11

Still, fair's fair. If Sandy wants to play Dr. Alexander Delacourt, socialite engineer, it probably doesn't hurt business. Nobody's better than Sandy at soft-soaping people like Ed, or whatever his name is. Besides, if Patrick and I hadn't broken up I wouldn't have been at the office either.

Sandy, still talking, had clapped Ed on the shoulder, but Ed, who had seemed enthralled, was letting his attention wander. His hand strayed to his tie as he gazed at a point beyond Marina's shoulder. "Mr. Bolton is here," he said.

The shrunken, frail-looking old man who got out of the limousine didn't look at all like the jolly gent with the straw hat and red nose who did the Fun World television commercials. On television Bobo, the clown-turned-entrepreneur, bounced and mugged. This Bobo—Mr. Bolton, chairman of the board of the Bolton Amusement Group—leaned heavily on the arm of the tall, blond man at his side. As he shuffled forward, the television lights illuminated his flyaway white hair and then caught the gleam of tears on his cheeks.

The little man waved away shouted questions as he approached. He ignored Ed's introduction and said, "My God, my God. Children. I love kids, and they love me. They always crowd around, and they say, 'Bobo—'" Shaking his head and mumbling, he moved to one side, to be replaced by the man who had helped him out of the car.

"Jack Sondergard, president of Fun World," the man said, extending his hand to Sandy. Sondergard looked about fifty. His face was thin, his blond hair graying. A nerve jumped near his eye but his voice was firm, and when he shook Marina's hand his palm was dry. After the handshake his eyes flicked over the top of Marina's head as he devoted his attention to Sandy.

Closed out, Marina found herself standing next to Bobo, who was wiping his face with a handkerchief. She edged away from him. The last thing I need is to be trapped by an old guy who isn't only senile but slobbering, even if he *is* the famous Bobo the Clown.

She had put an additional foot of distance between them before Bobo looked up and his faded brown eyes focused on her. "You're a lovely child," he said.

Caught. Maybe he'd rebury his face in his handkerchief. He didn't. "A lovely child," he repeated.

She stifled the impulse to tell him that thirty-two didn't qualify as a child in anybody's book, and as for lovely— well, even her mother, if she were alive, probably wouldn't go as far as *lovely*. "Thanks."

He took a step toward her. "What's your name?"

She sighed. He thinks I'm one of his kiddie fans. I'll tell him my name, and he'll tell me it's a very pretty name and ask me what grade I'm in. "Marina."

The old man didn't say what a pretty name it was. He swayed toward her with an air of confidentiality, putting a hand on her arm. "I knew a woman named Marina once. Knew her very well. We were on the road together back—my God, it must've been the twenties. She was an equestrienne. You know what an equestrienne is?"

"A bareback rider?"

"Very good. Marina Valdez. She had a silver-gray horse. Prince something. She wore blue, with silver spangles." His grip tightened. "We were close, Marina and I. Close. My God, she could ride."

Marina didn't answer. She was trying to catch the drift of the conversation between Sandy and Jack Sondergard. She heard Sondergard say something about "your top people."

"Do you like the circus, Marina?"

"Yes," she answered absently. "When we were kids, my sister and I—" She stopped, her face burning.

"What's your sister's name?"

How long had it been since she'd done that? Stupid, stupid. "Catherine."

Thank God he seemed to lose interest. She breathed deeply, willing her face to stop radiating heat, feeling a drop of perspiration sliding down between her breasts.

Tears began to trickle from his eyes again, and he dabbed at them with his handkerchief. "Children have been hurt, and it's my fault," he said.

She tilted her head back a little. Sandy was saying, "Give you every assurance—"

"We've always been so careful. Never a black mark, never. What happened?"

If Bobo got ticked off because she hadn't paid attention to him, Sandy wouldn't be pleased. "We'll find out."

"We?"

"The company I work for. Breakdown, Inc."

"What kind of company is that?"

So much for Sandy's publicity efforts. Give him the cocktail-party explanation. "We're engineers who investigate why things go wrong—plane crashes, nuclear power plant failures, why the gearshift lever knob comes off your car, anything."

He looked more alert. "How do you do that?"

14

On automatic pilot, she said, "Everything obeys physical laws—laws about speed, tension, impact, fatigue, things like that. We figure out which laws apply and why. Then we can figure out what caused the failure." And determine, she added silently, who was to blame for whatever smashed and should pay for it through the nose.

Straining to hear what Sondergard was saying about "results," she missed Bobo's next question. When she asked him to repeat it he said, "How will you find out what happened to Loopy Doop?"

His eyes were pleading. He wanted reassurance, but she wasn't about to spend half the night explaining Breakdown's procedures. She chose something relatively easy. "I might start by doing a fault tree."

"A fault tree?"

"It's a way of making sure the possibilities are covered."

"A tree? Like a family tree?"

She got out her notebook and pen and looked around. Better not talk about Loopy Doop. A Styrofoam cup lay at their feet. She pointed to it and said, "Here's an example. Suppose you pour hot coffee into that cup, and the coffee leaks out the bottom and scalds you badly. If I were making a fault tree, I'd put that at the top and we would call it the Most Undesired Event." She drew a rectangle at the top of the page and wrote in it "Leaky Cup."

He nodded. "What happened here tonight is the Most Undesired Event."

Keep him off Loopy Doop. "Right. Under the Most Undesired Event, I'd figure out what could have gone wrong with the cup. Maybe it's defective. Maybe it wasn't meant to hold hot liquid in the first place. Maybe it was damaged in shipping and there's a hole in the bottom. See?" She sketched in other rectangles. "Now, only one of those things has to go wrong to result in my Most Undesired Event, so I'll put a half a bullet here. We call that an Or gate. If it took more than one, I'd put an And gate—a dome shape."

He took a pair of Ben Franklin glasses from his pocket, put them on his nose, and gazed at her sketch. "Then what would you do?"

"I'd spread out from there, and put possible contributing factors under each possible cause. If the cup was damaged, was it damaged in shipping, or somewhere else? If it was the wrong kind of cup, was the order filled incorrectly, or was the wrong cup ordered? I'd go on until all the possibilities I could think of were exhausted. A single fault tree for a nuclear power plant could cover the floor of a room."

"When you finished, you'd know why I got scalded?"

"I'd know where to start looking."

"You could do that for the accident tonight?"

"Sure. I expect somebody will do one."

They were silent. Bobo took his glasses off and put them away. He drew a shuddering breath. "I'm an old man," he said. "In eighty-three years, this is the worst thing that has happened to me. My wife died of cancer. For that I could blame God. For this, I can only blame myself."

Marina closed her notebook, thinking she couldn't take much more of Bobo the Clown.

He twisted the hankerchief in his knobby hands.

"Marina, I must know. How can I rest in my grave if I don't know? You must find out for me."

"The company—"

"No, you. You." Abruptly, he pulled her forward, interrupting Sandy and Sondergard. "I want Marina to investigate this accident," he said.

Marina saw displeasure on Sondergard's face, and she knew Sandy saw it too. "Mr. Bolton, many people work on an investigation of this magnitude," Sandy said. "I can assure you—"

"She is the one who is to report to me," said Bobo. When he spoke in that tone, Marina thought, you could see traces of the whip-cracking executive he once must have been. "Is that understood?" He was looking at Sondergard.

Sondergard inclined his head.

Bobo seemed spent. Neither Sandy nor Sondergard looked at Marina. Marina wondered what Sandy would say later, when they were alone.


Marina's eyes watered from yawning as she adjusted the cross-section of Loopy Doop's leg in the hardness tester. Sandy had managed to get somebody out with a band saw, but she'd had to wait for the guy to show up and cut the tubing. After that, there had been the boring drive north on the freeway from Redwood City to San Francisco, a garish neon procession of motels, restaurants built of pseudowood or pseudostone and surrounded by vast parking lots, the airport, Candlestick Park on its gusty ocean promontory. At last the hills and the city— billboards advertising tequila, the Bank of America, the current show at Harrah's Tahoe, and beyond the bill-boards the angular, glittering high rises overlooking empty streets down which the wind, funneled between the glass-and-concrete sides of the buildings, blew fast and cold.

By the time she had taken the exit for the waterfront, the Bay Bridge looming ahead of her, it was nearly midnight. She drove past the Ferry building with its clock tower, a serene survivor of the 1906 quake now half-hidden by the Embarcadero Freeway, and parked her car a few hundred yards beyond.

The bay was rough. Water slopped against the pilings supporting the cavernous converted pier that housed the Breakdown offices. Carrying her chunks of round steel tubing in a plastic bag decorated with Bobo's laughing face, she let herself into the building.

She yawned again and wiped the corners of her eyes. Footsteps echoed across the pier's vast, open interior. Fernando, the security guard, making his rounds. She had already greeted him when she signed in at the front door, where he sat eating an apple and reading *Psychology Today*.

She elevated the platform until the steel touched a small penetrator attached to the gauge. Loopy Doop was hers—at least for the moment. So far, that had meant having to wait for the mechanic at Fun World while Sandy and Sondergard decamped in the Porsche and Bobo was trundled back to his Hillsborough estate in the limousine. It meant she was here doing a hardness test instead of at home getting some sleep.

Pushing the crank that would apply the load and cause the penetrator to dent the steel, she focused on the pointer. The hardness test was usually done first because it was quick and easy and didn't require a technician. Zip, zip, zip. Get the sample in, make the dent, take the load off, read the number, which was—she squinted—sixty-five on the Rockwell B scale. She wrote the figure in her notebook. The tensile strength test would have to wait until machined specimens could be made from the Loopy Doop sample and the chemical analysis would be sent to an outside lab, but at least this one was out of the way. Stifling yet another yawn, she took the specimen from the machine and tagged it for the evidence room.

The key to the evidence room was in its little magnetized box stuck under the overhang of the testing division secretary's desktop. She slid it out and, after making a notation on the sign-out sheet on the door, deposited Loopy Doop's fractured leg in one of the bins that lined the shelves inside.

As she was relocking the door the phone buzzed. She answered, and Sandy's voice said, "Thought I'd find you there. Listen. The teenagers—Wilson their name was, brother and sister—didn't make it. The ticket-booth lady and the mother probably will. It's touch and go with the little boy, but if he pulls through he'll be a quad."

"Uh oh."

"Yeah. Some other kids in line were hurt too, but he's the worst. This is going to be a hot little number."

"Looks like it."

"I don't need to tell you to keep your ass covered, do I?"

"Nope."

"Jack Sondergard isn't jumping for joy at what Bobo pulled on him. I'm a little surprised at the way you played that one."

"I didn't play anything. The old guy is just gaga."

"Right, right. We'll talk tomorrow. Sweet dreams."

Marina hung up. The stakes were rising. You couldn't collect more than a few hundred thousand for wrongful death, but a quadriplegic, especially a young one, was a different story. With a quad case, you were talking millions. And the insurance companies and Fun World and everybody else involved would be scrapping to make sure the millions didn't come out of their particular hides. They were all going to be very interested in what the investigation—her investigation—turned up. She switched off the overhead light and headed for home.


The man on the screen said, "Fun World is bankrolling the Loopy Doop investigation. Doesn't that make it more likely that you'll clear Fun World of blame?"

The woman on the screen looked disheveled, Marina thought, and tense in a twitchy, rabbity way. Why act so intimidated by that cut-rate Mike Wallace, she asked herself as the woman said, "Absolutely not. We've been hired to look for the truth. If our investigation shows that Fun World was negligent we'll not only tell them, we'll tell the world. We can't change the facts to favor one side over the other."

Sandy reached for his hamburger as the commercial started. "Fantastic, Marina. Perfect."

"I looked awful."

Sandy shook his head vigorously, his mouth full. When he'd swallowed, he said, "It's just like when you go on the witness stand. You don't want to look ultra-glamorous. People won't trust you." He turned to Don, his secretary, and said, "Isn't that right?"

Don was a marathon runner, with the runner's stringy, muscular body. He had green eyes and his head was covered with tight blond curls. He wore an aviator jacket and a narrow raspberry-colored tie and his feet, in battered running shoes, were propped on his desk. "I don't know," he said thoughtfully. "I think the white lab coat was a mistake. It made her look too pale."

"She was perfect."

Marina ran her hands through her hair. She had probably done the same thing, she realized, just before the interview, which was why it had been standing up like that. I *did* look pale. And rabbity. "I've got enough to do without worrying about looking like Miss America on the six o'clock news."

"That's what I just *said*." Sandy's tone was exaggeratedly patient. Turning to Don, he said in a mock-whisper, "Don't ever tell Marina she looks pale. Anything but pale."

"Got it," said Don. He proffered a greasy white bag to Marina. "Want a fry?"

"No thanks. Spoil my big dinner with Sondergard."

Sandy crumpled his napkin. "God. I forgot that was tonight. You'll have to talk to him, Don. I ate onions." He checked his watch. "When's he supposed to be here?"

"I told him about the news thing, and he said he'd stop by afterward to pick me up."

"Time enough to gargle."

As Sandy, straightening his tie, disappeared into the bathroom adjoining his office, Marina wondered again at how easily he seemed to have accepted Bobo's capricious insistence that she be given the Loopy Doop case. It was

21

she, after all, who'd been on the news, her picture—wearing the lab coat, staring through a microscope at nothing—that had been in the paper. When *People* magazine called, they'd asked for Marina Robinson. So had the wire services. It was the kind of attention Sandy loved, but he'd made no effort to do anything but coach from the sidelines. His attitude had given Marina some uneasy moments of wondering whether there was some reason he didn't want to be more closely involved himself.

On the other hand, it was opera season, the busiest time of his year, when he spent most evenings squiring this or that society grande dame or ingenue around to performances and parties. Despite the pictures that ran in the papers of Sandy with various women, both the women and anyone else who cared to know knew that Sandy's serious love for the past few years had been Don. Don hated opera, and refused to attend.

The phone buzzed, and Don sat up. "Your line, Marina." He answered, and raised his eyebrows at her as he punched the "hold" button. "It's Patrick."

"I'll go take it on my phone."

"But of course."

Marina stepped out of Sandy's office onto the open metal catwalk that surrounded it. Sandy's office was raised above the floor of the pier on metal supports and was accessible by a fire-escape staircase. As Marina descended to the main floor and walked past the glass-fronted office cubicles on the way to her own, she felt a headache forming behind her eyes. She and Patrick had agreed not to communicate. It had been his choice.

The red blink of the phone button was the only light in

her dim office. She sat down at her desk, picked up the receiver, and punched the button. "Patrick?"

"Hi." Music in the background, of course. A piece she couldn't quite recognize. He hesitated, then said, "I wanted to be sure you were all right."

"All right?"

"I've seen the stories in the papers. I just saw you on TV. There has to be a lot of pressure."

Just like Patrick. "I'm fine."

She heard him draw a long breath. "I was worried that this might be too much like—it might be too much."

"Too much like Palika Road?"

"That's what I meant, I guess."

Why couldn't he stay out of it? "Palika Road wasn't exactly an amusement-park ride."

Several bars of the music came through clearly, but she still didn't recognize it. Then he said, "I can't believe you didn't understand what I meant, so I guess you're being deliberately snotty."

Her cheeks were hot. "Listen. Catastrophes are my living. I can't afford to run screaming into the night when one happens." She swallowed. "You know that."

"Actually, I do know that. It was a feeble excuse to call you."

Neither of them spoke. Then she said, "How are things?"

"Not bad. At the store we're in the middle of the Christmas madness, selling lots of 'Jingle Bells' and the *Messiah*. The Sidewalk Symphony is making beautiful music except in the horn section. Lucy has dropped out."

"Not again."

"Yeah. She's doing some kind of bodywork, and her bodywork guy told her playing the horn was getting her spine out of alignment."

"That's Lucy, all right."

"It's really bad in the Vivaldi. Tanner's just not up to it. And speaking of bad news, it looks like the IRS or the FBI or somebody has finally caught up with me."

"What do you mean?"

"Guys calling the store to verify that I work there. And Mrs. Dobson told me she'd gotten a call to check that my address is really my address."

"They said they were from the IRS?"

"No. But what else?"

"Your taxes are OK, aren't they?"

"Except for my secret Swiss accounts, I am simply a record-and-tape-store manager and sometime orchestra conductor whose meager taxes are paid up to date."

"Once they crack your American account they'll realize they're wasting their time."

He chuckled. "No doubt."

The music had stopped. "I'd better go," she said.

"I love you, Marina."

She took a deep breath. "See you." She hung up.

She sat in her darkening cubicle, drumming her fingers on her desk. She could just make out, on the opposite wall, the photograph that looked like a lunar landscape but was really an electron-microscope view of corroded steel.

Patrick knew what was important to him. He might wear frayed sweaters and cords most of the time, but when his orchestra had a performance he showed up in a tux, and insisted that his musicians dress formally too.

His Berkeley apartment, in the flatlands off College Avenue, had almost no furniture, but was equipped with an elaborate stereo system and tape deck on which to play his huge collection of recorded music. He decided what was important to him, and he committed himself to it. It shouldn't have surprised her, then, that he had wanted to commit himself to her.

Which was the last thing she wanted. When he talked about living together, maybe getting married sometime, she felt numb. Worn out with it, pushed to the wall, she had compared her feelings to an alloy of metals: "Say this particular alloy is made to hold ten pounds of weight, OK? Its nature is to hold ten pounds. Put eleven pounds on it, and it breaks. It isn't made to hold eleven pounds."

"So what we've had together is ten pounds, and what I want is eleven pounds."

"Something like that."

"No matter how much I want it to, it won't hold eleven pounds."

"It *can't* hold eleven pounds, Patrick. It can't do it. It isn't made to do it. Don't you understand?"

"I understand what you're saying, but I don't believe it."

"Believe it."

Patrick was an optimist. He thought things could change. She was—not a pessimist, but a realist. Jack Sondergard was probably here by now. She'd take a minute to brush her hair and then she'd go.

\* \* \*

"Dessert?" Sondergard looked inquiringly at her as the waiter hovered.

She shook her head. "Just coffee."

"Two coffees." As the waiter moved off Sondergard drank the last of his wine and said, "Delicious."

Somewhat to Marina's surprise it *had* been delicious, and not all that unpleasant. She hadn't been sure what to expect when Sondergard invited her to dinner to discuss Loopy Doop, but had imagined the best she could hope for was an indifferent meal in a dim, half-empty hotel restaurant. Instead, Sondergard had brought her to one of the city's best fish places, where the lights were bright, the bar loud, smoky, and crowded with people drinking liquor instead of white wine, the booths dark wood and taller than head-height, the waiters middle-aged, and the menus printed every day. Sondergard had surprised her.

He had surprised her, too, by his cordial, even friendly manner. She had expected at least coldness, if not outright hostility, but ever since she had walked into Sandy's office to find him chatting with Don while Sandy took a phone call, Sondergard had been extremely nice. There were deep lines from his nose to his mouth, and light blue circles under his eyes, but these were the only evidence of strain. He had listened seriously while she explained, over dinner, the shape the investigation would take, and had asked questions that probed but didn't bully. He had even volunteered a few remarks about his wife and two teenaged children and had asked Marina why she'd wanted to be an engineer. As dinners with clients went it merited a pretty good rating. When coffee came, she leaned back, feeling her performance to be over, and started to relax.

Sondergard stirred his coffee, gazing into his cup. "I have to confess something to you."

Marina was instantly wary. She hated it when people said things like that. "Confess?"

He raised his eyes to hers and she felt a slight jolt of attraction. Watch out. "I'm afraid of what you might find," he said. "Scared to death."

She was speechless. He wasn't going to tell her how everything had been done by the book and he had nothing to hide? Didn't he know how the game was played? When she thought she could sound casual she said, "What are you talking about?"

He leaned forward. "You met my boss."

"You mean Bob—Mr. Bolton?"

"I mean Mr. Bolton. Do you have an idea of what I'm bucking?"

"I don't quite—"

"Let me explain. There are a hundred and fifty Fun Worlds in the country. I'm supposed to be in charge of them. Only I'm not, because nominally he is. Mr. Bolton is a wonderful old gentleman, and he started the company and God knows he should have a say, but—do you see what I'm getting at?"

"I think so."

"Hell, Marina—I hope I can call you Marina?—I spend half my time trying to uncover what he's done and fix it. He countermands my orders, wants to make sure cronies of his from way back stay on the payroll, goes over requisitions and decides five thousand of something will do instead of ten. I try to catch everything, but some of it's bound to slip by. And then—" He opened his long-fingered hands, palms upward.

"You mean he might've done something that led to the Loopy Doop collapse?"

"That's what I'm afraid of."

"But what?"

"I have no idea."

Marina stared at the few golden crumbs of sourdough crust littering the tablecloth.

"Listen." Sondergard's voice was husky. "I wouldn't let the old man take the blame. If the company's at fault, put it on me. That's how it should be. But still—I'm not anxious to go down the tubes for somebody else's mistake. Do you understand?"

His face was slightly flushed now, making his pale eyes and the shadows beneath them bluer. Marina nodded. "Sure."

"I don't know why I'm bringing it up, except to ask you to keep me closely informed. I know you'll be reporting to him, but I'd like you to stay in touch with me, too."

"I will."

Trying to digest what he'd said, Marina gazed at him. Instead of thinking about his remarks, though, she thought how good he looked. Spare and elegant, like Loopy Doop. No indication of need in his demeanor, nor of sloppy over-generosity. Exactly enough of everything.

Nothing could be easier, really, than for him to stop at her place and stay with her a while before going back to his wife and kids on the Peninsula. It might be pleasant, and it would be so much less draining and irritating than dealing with somebody like Patrick. She wondered briefly what Sondergard would say if she suggested it, then realized that he'd certainly say yes. Regretting that it wasn't going to happen, she sipped her coffee and found that it had gotten cold.

# STRESS

Parts break for one reason only: stress. That's an easy diagnosis and in the end an uninformative one, because there are many different kinds of stress. In metals, for example, a torn surface means overload. Wavy marks mean fatigue. Grains indicate corrosion. The way to identify the kind of stress a material has been under is to study the break closely.

*Why Breakdown?*

MARINA CURBED THE WHEELS AND GOT OUT OF the car into a pool of brightness from the street light. The narrow, winding street in the Berkeley hills was deserted. A light burned on the front porch of Clara's big, brown-shingled house. Marina stood for a moment, breathing the cold, foggy, eucalyptus-scented air, trying to clear her head before she crossed and rang the bell.

Her head wouldn't clear. When she blinked, she saw green numbers jumping on the insides of her eyelids—the numbers she'd been staring at on her computer terminal before she left the office. She tried not to blink, but her eyes burned and she blinked anyway.

The call from the boy's uncle hadn't helped—a stammering, embarrassing monologue about how she had to find the guilty party because when she did, the uncle would—well, he wouldn't say exactly what he was going to do, but—she wanted to scream at him to leave her alone, stop wasting her time. Not that she was doing much except wasting it herself.

Or Bobo was wasting it for her. He insisted on daily reports in person, and in order to be nearby he had taken a suite at the Mark Hopkins, on Nob Hill, instead of staying at home in Hillsborough. Every afternoon he had tea served for her in his little glass-walled, bubblelike solarium, and as she talked Marina had the sensation that she was floating over San Francisco, seeing the high rises of downtown, the hills, the bridges, the bay, from a detached, hermetically sealed height.

Bobo looked ravaged—his eyes red, his face doughy. Sometimes he seemed to be listening to what she said, but more often he was distracted. Occasionally he told her anecdotes about his early days with the circus, and Marina, thinking of the work waiting for her back at the office, bit down hard on the inside of her cheek as she nodded at him.

The little boy would live, a quadriplegic. The newspapers had printed a school picture showing a kid with floppy hair, a gap-toothed smile. She kept drawing a blank on his name, but it might be Tommy, or Ronnie. Agit. There was no reason to think about Agit More, and only somebody like Patrick, who understood nothing, would imagine there was. The uncle had been drinking, she thought. "Sweetest kid," he had said, "sister's little boy," and if he found out whose fault— When she closed her eyes this time she saw, instead of green numbers, smoke and flames.

Forget it. Forget it. Go talk to Clara. She started across the street toward the porch light.

Clara was, sometimes, Marina's therapist. The relationship had continued, off and on, since Marina had returned from India. When Marina felt she loathed and resented Clara to the point that she couldn't bear to look at her wizened little face, her ever-so-exquisite clothes, couldn't stand her superior, patronizing attitude any longer, she would stop seeing her for months or years. Eventually, Marina would call Clara and Clara would take her back with what seemed to Marina perfect indifference.

Now, Clara had almost given up her practice. Marina's sessions with her these days were more in the nature of visits. Each time Marina saw Clara, Clara looked more feeble. Marina resented that more than anything else—more than Clara's pushing and pushing her to talk about Halapur, and insisting that she say Catherine's name. When Marina saw Clara's hand quiver as she picked up a teacup, heard the fatigue in her low voice, she felt furious.

A few moments after she rang the bell, the door opened a crack and Mrs. Daughtry, Clara's nurse, peered out. Marina saw the glint of a security chain which hadn't been there before. "It *is* you," Mrs. Daughtry said, and unhooked the chain and stood back to let her in. As Marina walked down the polished hallway she heard the chain tinkle as Mrs. Daughtry slid it back into place.

Clara sat in front of the fire, tiny and gray, wearing a quilted jacket of printed yellow silk, an afghan tucked around her knees. The firelight was reflected in the beveled glass fronts of the bookcases, and flickered on the teapot and cups on the end table. When Clara poured, Marina saw the tremor and wondered if it was worse.

"I saw you on the news," Clara said.

"It's a big case. The biggest I've ever had." As always when she was with Clara, Marina felt herself starting to talk fast, rushing to get everything said. Usually, Clara's attention was obviously focused on Marina. Tonight, though, Marina thought Clara's mind was on something else.

When Marina finished talking about Loopy Doop, Clara leaned her head against the back of her chair and closed her eyes. Disconcerted, Marina said nothing. After a few moments, Clara said, "I had a shock. It has left me feeling—very bad. Someone broke into my house."

The idea of an intruder here, among the books, the lemon-scented wood, the ceramic vases, was unsettling. "Was anything stolen?"

"Nothing at all. I'm sure I wasn't supposed to know anyone had been here. I was asleep upstairs, and Mrs. Daughtry had gone out for the afternoon."

"What happened? Did you hear somebody?"

"I heard nothing. I only realized someone had been here because, as you know, I lead an extremely orderly life. I recognize it as an obsession, of course." Clara smiled self-deprecatingly. "You probably remember that on the desk in my office there is a crystal paperweight on an ebony stand. The stand is really a box, where I keep the keys to my desk and my filing cabinet. When I came down later in the afternoon, I saw immediately that the paperweight and stand had been moved. They weren't moved far, you understand. But moved."

"But couldn't Mrs.—"

33

"She never goes into my office, and besides, she says not. She was away, in any case, and had it been disturbed earlier I would have noticed. Once I did notice, I saw other things as well. Some disarrangement of the materials in my desk drawers. Scratches where someone forced the lock to get into the room through the sliding glass doors."

"Did you call the police?"

"I called the police, and I called the locksmith. The police came, they looked, but there is nothing they can do. Nothing was stolen, after all. The Berkeley police have worse crimes to think about.

"The locksmith accomplished more. He put on new locks, and chains, and some sort of bar device on the glass doors to make it more difficult the next time someone wants to intrude."

The bitterness in Clara's voice was evident. She sighed. "It's the times, I suppose. I'm not the only one. There's talk of forming some sort of block association. I'm lucky I didn't lose anything."

"Why do you suppose nothing was taken?"

"Perhaps the person was frightened off. Or perhaps it was an estranged husband, snooping in his wife's file for ammunition to use in a divorce, and he found what he needed. Perhaps anything."

When Marina left Clara's the fog had come down through the eucalyptus trees and settled around the house. The street lamps were smudges of light that illuminated nothing. The neighborhood—a neighborhood of teenagers, and well-fed cats, and Berkeley professors, and little girls who took dancing lessons— seemed alien, peopled by beings who came and went without invitation or warning and left disquiet behind them. Clara would lie in her bed tonight wondering if they would return. Marina slammed her car door hard, because she wanted to make a noise.

"Hold on," the attendant said, and the safety bar descended over Marina's knees and then over Jack Sondergard's knees next to hers. Across the empty park Marina could see "Season's Greetings" spelled out in colored lights over the entrance. The manager of the Seattle Fun World, hunched in his raincoat by the ticket booth, was gazing at the sky, which looked as if another drizzle might start any minute. Marina had always heard that it rained all the time in Seattle, and nothing in the several hours she'd been here had disproved it. On the drive from the airport, half-listening to the Seattle manager chatting nervously with Sondergard—Jack, he'd insisted she call him—she watched the magnificent green of the landscape through a haze of droplets.

Maybe a trip to Seattle hadn't been strictly necessary. Certainly it hadn't been necessary for Sondergard—Jack—to accompany her. His decision to do so had thrown her off a little, but on the other hand he was paying for the tickets.

"I've looked over the records. Loopy Doops have to be inspected annually for cracks and flaws," she had told Sandy and Sondergard at their most recent meeting in Sandy's office. "What I don't understand is"—she ran her finger down the list—"the older machines, the ones that have been in service longest, have perfect records. No fatigue failures, no bends, not even a hint. On the other hand, the Redwood City Loopy Doop, which was

so new it hadn't even been through an annual inspection
yet—"

The phone buzzed and Don, who had been taking
notes, said "Dammit" and went to answer.

Sondergard leaned forward. "You're saying—"

"I'm saying I think the Loopy Doop leg broke because
of low-cycle fatigue, yet there's no initial flaw, and it had
been operating less than a year. The older machines not
only haven't broken, they don't show any danger signals.
It's strange."

Don returned and said, "The kids's uncle again, for
Marina. I told him she was out."

"Christ," said Sandy.

"If he calls again," Marina said, her eyes still on the
inspection list, "tell him I've gone to—to Seattle."

Perhaps it wasn't necessary to ride Loopy Doop either,
but it had seemed a natural outgrowth of looking at it,
poking around in its engine, and running her hand along
the cold, damp steel legs that showed no sign of bending.

Sitting in the gondola, though, with Sondergard's
shoulder pressing against hers, waiting for the attendant
to start the engine, she needed to swallow several times.
This ride has operated three years without anyone getting
even a scraped knuckle, she told herself, and swallowed
again.

The jangly music was starting, and she could feel the
effect of having the legs so thin. It gave the ride a
wavery, springy feel that was already making her hands
clammy, and as the gondola started to swoop upward she
had to stifle a scream. She glanced sideways at Sondergard, and although he looked impassive she saw that he
was clutching the bar convulsively.

The gondola descended again, fast, and her nose

started to run. She dug in her jacket pocket, hoping for a tissue, and luckily found one. When had she felt like this? She squeezed her eyes shut as the gondola reared upward as if to fling them into the grove of evergreens at the edge of the park. Maybe this was how they had felt, the two chubby teenagers who'd gone plummeting down into the ticket booth. The music loud like this, a tune that pulled at her nerves with every jagged bar. She pressed the tissue to her streaming nose, then wiped her eyes on her sleeve. She had to stop acting so outrageously stupid. She blew her nose and glanced at Sondergard again, just catching him shifting his eyes away from her.

That was enough to put her back in control. For the rest of the ride she clung to the bar and managed, she thought, to look calm as the world tossed around her and Loopy Doop performed perfectly. When she climbed out of the gondola, though, her legs wobbled and nearly gave, and she clutched the edge of the car to steady herself. Holding onto it, she noticed something. She studied a scratch on the gondola's metal side, pulled a pencil-like magnet from her "doctor bag," then turned to Sondergard. "This is aluminum."

Sondergard's face was very white. He shrugged slightly. "Oh?"

"The gondolas for the Redwood City Loopy Doop are steel."

He was patting his brow with a handkerchief. "What's the difference?"

"Well—weight for one thing—the main thing. Steel is heavier."

"You mean the gondolas on the other ride—"

"Were heavier, that's all. Maybe a hundred pounds."

"Couldn't that have made the difference—"

"I doubt it. It's funny that it was changed, though. You don't know anything about it?"

She watched a crease deepen between his brows. "I can't swear I hadn't heard about it, but right now—I don't think so."

"I'll take another look at the specifications when I get back."

The drizzle started. She felt Sondergard's hand on her back as he guided her toward the waiting limousine, where the Seattle manager had already taken shelter. The Loopy Doop attendant, standing neaby, said, "What did you think, Mr. Sondergard?"

Sondergard shook his head. "Too much for me."

"Just as well you shut that one down. Nobody would ride it anyway, now. Except on a dare."

They got into the limousine, and Sondergard told the driver to take them to the airport. The Loopy Doop ride had silenced everybody, even the Seattle manager. Marina gazed out the window at the darkening landscape and listened to the click of the windshield wipers and the hiss of the tires on the freeway. By the time they reached the airport, she had almost stopped shaking.


Bobo patted his mouth with a napkin printed with a sprig of holly. His eyes were vague. "I don't understand," he said.

Of course not. Marina cleared her throat. "What I was asking," she said, raising her voice and speaking slowly, "was whether you knew anything about this decision to change from aluminum to steel gondolas in the Loopy Doop rides."

She waited. Bobo patted his mouth a few more times. She plowed on. "The specifications say that a little over a year ago Fun World didn't renew a contract for aluminum gondolas that you had with Gonzales Manufacturing in Fremont. You now get steel gondolas, and all your specialty steel, from Singapore Metal Works, in Singapore." She was practically yelling. Out near Alcatraz, a barge wallowed laboriously, slowly, through choppy green water. That was what it was like to deal with Bobo.

Bobo's distant look, however, had been replaced by a more thoughtful one. "Gonzales? Al Gonzales?" he said.

"I don't know the first name. It's in Fremont."

"Sure. Al Gonzales. Took me out to the best Mexican dinner I ever ate. Al does some work for me."

He was out of it, but what else was new? "Not any more. Gonzales Manufacturing lost the contract over a year ago. The new supplier is Singapore Metal Works."

Bobo rubbed a spot in the middle of his forehead, his eyes closed. "That can't be right. I would never dump Al. Nobody talked to me about it."

"Maybe they didn't want to—"

Bobo turned abruptly and barked, "Pete!" He looked almost animated. A young man with razor-cut hair, one of the several Fun World employees who were always around, appeared. Bobo said, "What's this about you boys dumping Al Gonzales?"

"I don't know what you mean, Mr.—"

"Find out. And bring me a report."

As Pete disappeared, Bobo said, "Al Gonzales bought me the best margarita I ever drank. The best . . ."

His voice trailed off, and Marina gathered her things. Another exercise in futility. She doubted it was significant, anyway.

Talking to Bobo was something to do during the Christmas doldrums, at least, while everything else came to a standstill. Tensile tests on Loopy Doop's steel couldn't be done, because the machined specimens couldn't be made, because half the technicians were on vacation. The chemical analysis couldn't be done because the laboratory's Christmas party was apparently using up everybody's energies.

In the meantime, nobody but Marina seemed to think any of this was urgent. "Hell, the suits haven't even been filed. All the lawyers are off skiing," said Sandy, who, naturally, was preoccupied with keeping his tuxedo in good shape and other matters of significance.

Even Sondergard, when she ran into him in Sandy's office one day talking with Don, said, "Listen—give it till after New Year's."

"It's falling on deaf ears, Jack. Marina's the original Scrooge," Don said.

Marina grimaced. It wasn't that she disliked Christmas, it was that she could never understand why, when there was work to be done, everybody should tacitly agree that things could come to a standstill for three solid weeks. Sure, have parties, give presents if you had anybody to give them to, but—it was useless to complain. She couldn't change the situation, so she might as well do something silly like drive down to Fremont and visit Gonzales Manufacturing.

With a feeling of playing hooky, she drove out of the parking garage, headed down Nob Hill on California

Street, and took Battery toward the Bay Bridge. The city was jammed with shoppers, and trees blinked everywhere. By the time she returned from Fremont it would be too late to go back to the office. As an extra bonus, the Christmas party was this afternoon, and she'd miss it.

The midafternoon traffic on the Bay Bridge was light, and as she drove she thought about the switch from aluminum to steel gondolas. It probably wasn't important, but it was curious. When you had a design that in any case depended on thin legs of high strength steel, why give the legs extra weight to carry, even if they could carry it easily? She'd ask Sondergard about it again, in case he'd remembered something.

She made good time, and in forty minutes was taking the exit closest to the industrial park where, she had learned from the map, she would find the street Gonzales Manufacturing was on. The way led through wide, anonymous streets strung with plastic Santas and lined with taco stands and used-car dealerships. She turned off into the industrial park with its rows of small, anonymous factories of beige- or cream-colored concrete, the newer ones landscaped with spindly young trees.

Gonzales was in an older section, and the only things growing near it were blackberries forcing their way through cracks in the empty parking lot. Marina left her car beside the weathered redwood sign with "Gonzales Manufacturing" painted on it in yellow and walked to the front door. A heavy bar lock and chain hung across it. Peering through the glass, she could glimpse part of an empty office and a bare gray metal desk. Apparently Gonzales wasn't manufacturing anything these days.

The factory next door was still in business. Marina

walked across the parking lot to it. A dark-haired young woman, sitting behind a receptionist's desk covered with standing Christmas cards, glanced up as she entered.

"I was just over at Gonzales," Marina said. "Where've they gone?"

The girl shrugged. "Closed down."

"When?"

"Couple of months ago, I guess."

"Do you know where I could find Mr. Gonzales, who used to run the company?"

The girl shook her head. "I don't know anything about it." She hesitated. Marina didn't move. After a moment the girl said, "We hired their foreman. He can probably tell you."

Marina had learned that standing her ground a little longer than was strictly polite often got results. She said, "I'd like to speak with him for a minute."

Gonzales's former foreman was a graying man in his fifties, dressed in khaki. Marina told him who she was. When she mentioned Fun World, his face hardened. "If it wasn't for those bastards, Gonzales would still be in business," he said. "The only good that came out of it was, at least we weren't involved in that accident. But when Fun World didn't renew the contract, that was it. A lot of good people out on the street. I was lucky, got another job. Not like some of the rest of them."

"Gonzales closed down because of Fun World?"

"Not exactly." He rubbed his hands over his face. "We were in trouble already. It was the straw that broke the camel's back, if you know what I mean."

"What happened to Mr. Gonzales?"

"Enrique? I think he's still trying to pick up the pieces.

He's got an office in the Fremont Plaza building, downtown."

"Actually, I meant Al."

"Oh. The old man died right after the plant went belly-up. Stroke, or something. Shame."


Enrique Gonzales tapped a piece of paper with his pencil point, gazing out the window of the tiny office. "I just wish my father hadn't lived to see the day, that's all," he said.

Marina didn't reply. The atmosphere in the room was oppressive with Enrique Gonzales's anger.

"I swear to God," Gonzales said. "Sometimes I think that accident is God's way of punishing Fun World for what they did to us. Let *them* find out what it's like to struggle. Let *them* feel shame." He turned back to Marina. He was a solidly built man in rolled-up shirt sleeves, with a broad face. A lock of straight black hair fell over his forehead. "There was never any trouble with anything we did for them. We worked with them for years. From Bobo's very first park. My father and Bobo—" He held up two fingers pressed together. "Then they pull the rug out from under us and take their business to Singapore."

"Nobody said why?"

"Not a word. After all those years. My father, sick as he was, tried to get Bobo on the phone. The secretary said Bobo was unavailable." Gonzales gave the last word a bitter twist.

"Why do you think—"

"Money, lady." Gonzales's lip curled. "Don't you know that's what everything's about? What do they live on over in Singapore, rice or something? They don't have to pay wages like we do here. Unemployment? Workmen's comp? They never heard of it.''

He had a point. Still, why not get aluminum gondolas made in Singapore, instead of steel ones? "Thanks," she said.

"I pray for the ones who died, for the ones who were hurt," Gonzales said. "But to see Fun World in trouble— It's the only thing that keeps me going."

Marina stood up, anxious to get away. She left him bent over the desk, writing numbers on a sheet of paper.

The letter arrived the day of a storm—another in a procession of storms that started at Christmas, continued through New Year's, and showed no sign of ending. Marina was almost accustomed, by now, to waking up in the early morning to the sound of spitting rain and, in the evening, creeping home with her headlights illuminating the downpour, always hoping her car or somebody else's wouldn't skid on a hill.

When, damp and tired, she opened the mailbox in the lobby of her apartment building and her fingers touched the onionskin envelope, she felt the same flash of irritation she used to feel and the accompanying thought: a letter from Catherine. She wasn't even surprised to see the Indian stamps, the Bombay postmark. An instant later, her mouth filled with bitter fluid and she sat down abruptly on the concrete ledge of the planter next to the mailboxes. She put the letter on her knee. Her name and address, typed with a faint ribbon. No return address. Don't sit looking at it, open it.

The single sheet of onionskin rustled as she tried to unfold it. The typed message was brief:

*Rain Sister,*
   *You told me trees write stories on the sky and only you can read them. What do the trees tell you now? Can you read the sky?*
                              *Cloud Sister*


She stared at the spongy green moss in the planter. She must have been about seven then, and Catherine four. They were kneeling on the bed, looking out the window at bare winter limbs. "The ends of the branches are pencils," Marina had said, her breath condensing on the cold glass, and she "read" to Catherine the story written on the sky, repeating something from a book the teacher had read at school. Catherine listened, rapt, her eyes huge and blue. After that she had often asked Marina to read what the trees had written.

Rain Sister and Cloud Sister. What had that game been about? They had played it over and over. To become Rain Sister she had wrapped herself in their mother's fringed gray silk shawl with its border of pink roses. Catherine, Cloud Sister, had worn a white angora sweater.

She'd been sitting here a long time. She got up stiffly and took the elevator to her apartment.

Catherine was dead. She had died ten years ago, when the Palika Road ashram burned—was burned, after the sacrifice of Agit More. Marina put the letter on the kitchen table and walked, hugging her elbows, through her low-ceilinged, anonymous apartment, with its bare white walls, its expanses of glass overlooking rain-slick streets and in the distance beyond the lights the black stretch of the bay. She went back to the table and picked up the letter.

It couldn't be from Catherine, because Catherine was dead. She tried to avoid the thought that she hadn't actually seen Catherine's body. There had been no body to see. Neither Catherine's nor those of the two other members of the faithful who refused to desert Nagarajan no matter what atrocities he'd committed. She had seen Catherine's ring, which the police had found, along with the bones and teeth of three people, after the ashes cooled. The ring, a bauble picked up for a few rupees in some bazaar, was twisted, but by some fluke not entirely melted, and it had a pink stone. She could see it, lying in the light from the desk lamp, and she could smell the bureaucratic police-station smell of paper crumbling, year after year, in the damp heat. They had asked, tentatively, if she wanted to keep the ring. When she said no, they put it carefully in a small brown envelope which had probably long since disintegrated in its turn.

By that time Nagarajan had hanged himself in his jail cell, and there was little to do but come home, despite the threats of the parents of the other victims and some posturing by the government. Even then, Marina had seen irony in the king cobra strangling himself. Unless he actually had been beaten to death by the police, a distinct possibility. Nobody had been left but Marina, who hadn't wanted to be there in the first place, who had come to India only because that was where Catherine was, and she was responsible for Catherine. She had flown to Bombay full of determination to regain her sister. She had left with nothing, not even Catherine's ring.

Catherine was dead, so this letter couldn't be from Catherine. It was like Catherine, though, to be so cryptic. To jerk Marina around, just to prove she still could.

When Marina had gotten back from India, she had thrown out or given away everything that belonged to Catherine—her Western clothes, which she'd long since given up wearing; her school notebooks; the pictures she'd drawn when she was a child. Because if Catherine had done what Marina wanted and gone back to school instead of getting mixed up with Nagarajan and going to India, she would be alive. It was Catherine's fault. But it was Marina's fault, because Marina was responsible for Catherine. How many times had Marina gone around on that wheel?

Their parents' death, in an airplane crash on the way to a football game in Los Angeles, had been Marina's introduction to disaster. She was eighteen when it happened, and was getting ready to start her freshman year at Stanford. Catherine was fifteen. Two orphans with few relatives, and those far away. It seemed best to everyone that she and Catherine do what they preferred—continue living in the little house in the Avenues near Golden Gate Park where they had grown up. Marina forgot Stanford and enrolled in San Francisco State.

For several years, it worked. It was fine. They shared household tasks, got decent grades, worked at part-time jobs to supplement the insurance money. Once the initial shock of bereavement wore off, they were—Marina was, anyway—reasonably happy.

Catherine apparently wasn't. How else to explain her rejection of their life together, in her first year at State, in favor of placing herself in the hands of Nagarajan, a two-bit guru whom even the gurus had never heard of? At the time, in the early seventies, there were dozens of Indian saints, Tibetan saints, Chinese and Japanese living gods, yogis, boddhisattvas, Sufis, dervishes, you name it running around San Francisco and Berkeley establishing ashrams, temples, meditation halls, giving lectures, classes, intensives. Everybody was seeking the Way and the Path. So Marina simply laughed and kidded Catherine when Catherine hung the photograph of Nagarajan in her room and put fresh flowers in front of it every day.

It took a long time for Marina to realize it was serious. She had worried from time to time that Catherine might get pregnant or become a drug addict, but something like this had never occurred to her. One afternoon when Catherine wasn't home, Marina went in to look at the picture. Catherine's room smelled of incense. A brightly printed Indian cotton spread covered her bed.

The picture of Nagarajan hung over the incense burner. It was in color, heavily and too brightly retouched. It showed, from the waist up, a slim young Indian man with prominent facial bones and large, dark eyes. Curly, luxuriant black hair hung to his shoulders. His bare brown chest was smooth and muscular, and his lips, half-smiling, were full and well-molded and looked, to Marina, almost feminine. Behind his head was a chair or a piece of sculpture shaped like an umbrella of golden cobras with their hoods flared open.

When Marina looked at the picture she felt, for the first time, dread at what might happen to Catherine. Despite its tackiness, she couldn't scoff at it.

"The nagas were ancient Indian gods," Catherine said when Marina questioned her later. "They can take the form of humans or snakes. A *nagarajan* is a naga king."

"How did this guy get to be a *nagarajan*?"

"He had a wise teacher, who recognized that he was one."

Marina wanted to take Catherine by the shoulders and shake her until her teeth rattled. "Are you telling me you believe that? You believe this guy is a snake-god in human form? Do you know what Freud would say about all this snake business?"

"I believe in Nagarajan, yes. Yes."

"But Catherine—" Catherine was so beautiful, Marina thought, with her long, shining yellow hair disarranged by the vehemence of her affirmative nod, looking flushed and embattled and resolute. "You've never even seen Nagarajan himself. How can you say you believe in him?"

"I've felt his spirit."

"What does he teach, or preach, or whatever?"

"That we are one, and the universe is one, and we must be what we are."

"That's fine, that's fine, that's all very well, but—"

Catherine touched Marina's cheek. "If your mind is closed, how can you possibly understand? Why don't you come to a meditation service with me?"

Marina went, following the theory that she had to know her enemy. She felt ill at ease beforehand, despite Catherine's touching eagerness for her to approve of everything. Some gurus, Marina knew, had wealthy devotees who remodeled mansions for their headquarters. That was evidently not the case with Nagarajan. The next evening Catherine took her to a storefront in the Tenderloin, wedged between an alcoholic rehabilitation center and a pornographic bookstore. Banner-sized posters of Nagarajan, the same photograph that hung in Catherine's room, were plastered on the dusty, smeared

49

windows. Young Americans in robes and saris greeted them. Incense was burned, the small company swayed and chanted. The ritual carried out in the bare, seedy-looking little room seemed harmless enough—or would have seemed so, if it hadn't been for Nagarajan's image on the wall.

Watching Catherine's ecstatic response as she chanted and swayed, her eyes closed, smiling, Marina felt closed off and bereft. Afterward, Catherine pressed her for a reaction: "Did you feel the vibrations? Wasn't it terrific?"

"Well, sure. It was really interesting."

"You didn't feel it. You didn't feel anything."

"I don't think I felt exactly what *you* feel, but—"

After that, Catherine had not invited her again.

*What do the trees tell you now? Can you read the sky?* It was suffocating in here. She blotted her upper lip with the back of her hand and realized she was still wearing her raincoat. She took it off and turned down the thermostat. *Can you read the sky?* No. She closed the curtains.

Yet as she watched the cloth swing and settle in front of the windows something exploded in her body—a blinding throb of pain or joy. Catherine. As beautiful, as impossible, as infuriating as ever. Marina heard with astonishment her own gasping, breathless laugh. Catherine again. She giggled, and pressed her hands against her mouth to cut off the absurd sound while her body continued to quiver. She had to bite down on her fingers before she could stop.

Hiccuping, she sat on the couch. The couch felt different—the rough, nubby texture of its cover almost

50

insupportable against the backs of her legs, the palms of her hands. If Catherine wrote, she doesn't hate me. If Catherine wrote— The thing I keep forgetting is that Catherine's dead.

Marina was tired, almost too tired to move. She leaned her head back and closed her eyes. If Catherine's dead, then who wrote the letter? Catherine. No. If Catherine's dead, who wrote the letter? Catherine. No.

A joke or something. You couldn't trace a letter like that. I don't even know anybody in Bombay. Except Catherine. Except—except I do know somebody in Bombay. Joginder was in Bombay, or he had been ten years ago. She had had the taxi go there on the way to the airport, weaving through the narrow streets looking for Joginder's brother's house. Somehow, they had found the street in a warren of tin-roofed huts, and a teenaged boy, shorts flapping around his thin legs, had led them to Joginder. She had tried to thank him, tried to give him money.

She didn't know the address, or if she could find the place again.

Find the place again.

She sat up. The letter was still in her hand. She held it away from her body while she went to the hall closet. She stuffed it in a shoebox that contained paid bills from past years and slid the box to the back of the closet shelf. Now it was gone.

# FAILURE

Failures will occur. It's inevitable. We can even calculate, by multiplying frequency and severity, the total risk—or cost, in the largest sense—of failure. On a continuum of severity of safety failures, at one end we would put a failure that resulted in no injury. At the other end, we would put a failure that resulted in death.

*Why Breakdown?*

MARINA'S EYES SLID FROM THE SHEET OF SPECI-fications back to the screen. The specifications said Loopy Doop was made of heat-treated 4140 steel. The yield strength—the amount of pressure that would make the steel bend—was 125,000 pounds per square inch. The ultimate strength, the point where the steel would break under pressure, was 140,000 pounds per square inch.

Plenty of safety margin, even with steel gondolas. Loads would be only a quarter to a fifth of the strength.

Why, then, did she have a hardness number of sixty-five on the Rockwell B scale? No 4140 steel would give such a low reading. Something was strange.

If the steel really was that soft, the weight of the

gondolas could have been a factor in the break. She felt a spurt of elation. Sure. Weak steel, an extra load—it might work. She might have the loose thread she needed to unravel the case.

First, she had to find out exactly what the steel was. Results of the other tests would tell her for sure. She dialed the testing division. The voice on the other end said, "The Loopy Doop tensile test? I know the specimens were made. I saw them around yesterday."

She spoke with exaggerated politeness. "If you happen to run across them again maybe you could run them for me and get them out of your way?"

The voice was unrepentant. "Glad to. I'll call you."

Next, she called Don. "Haven't seen a thing," he said when she asked about the chemical analysis. "I'll get in touch with the lab and tell them to step it up."

"Thanks."

"You sound a little weird. Is anything wrong?"

"Oh—I noticed something that doesn't check out, that's all."

"I'll get back to you after I talk to them."

Marina hung up. Is anything wrong? Just a few nightmares. She had been standing in a gray fog, and Catherine's ash-covered figure rose up in front of her. She'd woken up drenched with sweat, the way she used to in India—wet, thirsty, wrung out with needs she couldn't understand or control. Is anything wrong? What a question.

She told Clara. Of the dreams, Clara said, "The sleeping dragons have awakened."

"I didn't think they were sleeping. I thought they were dead."

"They don't die. They will not leave you. But they may change their form."

"I want them dead."

"When you realize that they are you, I think you will prefer to have them live."

Clara seemed woozy, and acted as if speaking were an effort. Marina wondered what drugs she was taking.

Sixty-five on the Rockwell B. She'd have to look up— The phone buzzed, and Don said, "The lab will messenger the report over tomorrow—the day after at the latest. And Jack's on the phone. He wants to know if you're free for lunch."

"Well—sure. I guess so."

"He said if you said yes, tell you he'd be by at twelve-thirty."

So she'd have the test results in a couple of days, and then everything would be squared away. In the meantime, she had to concentrate, sharpen up. She remembered Bobo asking one of his razor-cut flunkies to look into why Fun World had canceled their contract with Gonzales Manufacturing and switched to gondolas from Singapore. Probably nothing had been done, and Bobo had forgotten about it two minutes later. Still, if he hadn't— She started to pick up the phone, then rested her hand on the receiver. Talking to Bobo in person was hard enough. Talking to him on the phone, she had discovered the couple of times she'd tried to avoid a personal meeting, was impossible. She checked her watch. She just had time to run to the Mark Hopkins and see him before lunch with Jack.

When she called his room from the lobby, though, the smooth-sounding man who answered the phone stayed off the line a very long time. She heard his quiet voice, punctuated by querulous-sounding retorts from Bobo that finally got loud enough for her to hear, or to think she heard, "For God's sake, what does *she* want?"

Screw you too, she thought, not quite suppressing a flicker of dismay. This wasn't how it was supposed to go. Bobo had wanted to see her, had insisted on it. He would have nobody but her in charge of the case. Maybe she hadn't heard right. In any case, the volume of the conversation lowered and a moment later the smooth voice told her to come up.

Bobo did not, as he always had, struggle to his feet when she entered the solarium. He remained slumped in his rattan chair, looking at her with red eyes that were almost lost in the wrinkles around them. He hadn't shaved, and the late-morning light picked out every hair of the white stubble on his cheeks and chin. His stare seemed distracted and hostile at once, and she wondered if he knew exactly who she was. When he didn't ask her to sit down, she balanced on the edge of a chair.

She was deciding whether to broach the subject of Gonzales Manufacturing or give up and leave when he said, "Make a good thing out of this business, don't you?"

"What?"

"It's how people are today. Professionalism, loyalty—" The hand with which he waved away the rest of his remark was shaking.

Great idea to come here. Great move. "I don't understand."

He muttered something in a tone so low she couldn't make out the words.

She stood up. "I'd better go."

"No, no, no." He must've had one of his turnabouts from irrational to rational, because the glance he shot at her was keen. "What can I help you with, little lady?" The sarcastic tone wasn't her imagination.

By the time she explained about Gonzales and Singapore and the steel, he was drifting. "The steel might be too soft—much softer than it should've been. You'd asked somebody to investigate why the contract was canceled, so I thought . . ." she let her voice trail off, watching him rub his hands over his face in obvious confusion.

"I'll see about it," he said distantly. As she left, she heard him ask, "Isn't that Al Gonzales? With the margaritas?" She didn't answer.

She was losing ground, she thought as she drove back to the office. She watched the traffic intently, feeling that any moment a bus, a truck could demolish her. Bobo had acted angry, but it was impossible to know whether he was angry at something that had happened today or twenty years ago. It would've seemed simple enough, though, to keep at least this on the rails. At least this, if nothing else.

Sondergard took her to an Italian place—all red tile, chrome, natural wood, and white walls—near the opera house. He looked thinner, and his blond hair was now more obviously shot through with silver. His appearance seemed refined, somehow. The edges were obvious, the angles barely hidden. They drank Bloody Marys and he said, "The first suit is about to be filed. Six million dollars on behalf of the little boy."

"That's just the beginning."

"Sure. They'll be flying thick and fast now." He

consulted the menu. "Pasta? The linguine with clams is pretty good here."

The suits would come in and the insurance companies would scream and Fun World would be looking for a scapegoat in its turn. "There's one thing I'm looking into—a chance you've been sold inferior steel."

He put his glass down. "What are you talking about?"

"A test I did indicates that Loopy Doop may have been made out of steel much softer than it should be. I'm waiting for confirmation now. If it turns out to be true, you might have a case against Singapore Metal Works."

His fingers felt cool against the back of her hand. "Do you mean it? Are you sure?"

"Yes, I mean it. No, I'm not sure."

His fingers tightened. "Do you realize this could get us off the hook? If it turns out Singapore was screwing us—"

She felt warm, almost too warm. After her unpleasant encounter with Bobo, Sondergard's intimacy was working on her body like a balm. "Look. I shouldn't have said anything. The tests—"

He turned her hand over and kissed her palm. When his lips touched her skin she felt a ripple of shock. "Thank you," he said.

There was another thing, something she hadn't thought of until now. "If it turns out the steel was substituted and somebody in the company knew—"

"Oh God. You mean Bobo."

"It just occurred to me. I had a very strange meeting with him this morning. Something seemed to be wrong, and I can't figure out what it is."

"Now you see what it's like to work for him. That's the story of my life."

"Actually, when I talked to him about it before, he said he didn't know anything about Singapore Metal. He was really surprised when I told him Gonzales Manufacturing had lost the contract for the gondolas."

Sondergard shook his head. "That was the story when he told it to you, sure. And if you talked to him today, he might tell you the opposite. Believe me. You haven't dealt with him as much as I have."

The palm of her hand seemed to be pulsing. She was intensely aware that his fingers were still laced with hers. "Anyway," he was saying, "the specifications haven't been changed, have they?"

When she shook her head he said, "We may be out of the woods then, anyway, if we specified hard steel and they gave us some lousy alloy."

"But listen, Jack. I may be wrong. The tests aren't complete."

"Not you, Marina. You wouldn't ever be wrong." He smiled exultantly. "I know you wouldn't."

Marina never went to bed with clients, and it was with a kind of vertigo that, in his car after lunch, she found herself clinging to Jack Sondergard, returning his kisses, burning.

Dazed with shock and desire, she told him how to get to her apartment. In bed, she held him tightly, fervently, as if she could never get close enough.

She watched him dress later, in the fading light of approaching evening, watched him tie his tie, shake out his jacket, comb his silvery-blond hair. Her hair and the sheet beneath her were damp with sweat. She was thirsty.

He bent over her and kissed her. "Let me know about those tests, OK?" he said, and when she nodded he left.

In the first moments after he was gone she lay still,

barely breathing, waiting for the first lash of self-contempt.

It was a bad night. Marina lay wide-eyed in the darkness, unable even to hope for sleep, unable to connect a train of thought. Sometimes she would forget her episode with Sondergard, then remember it suddenly, her stomach clenching each time. Toward daybreak she dozed, and woke convinced that Nagarajan was in the room. His spicy smell still in her nostrils, she sat up and looked around, terrified. The feeling persisted so strongly that she put on her bathrobe and walked through the apartment, searching. Slightly calmed by its bland, everyday emptiness, she took a shower and got ready for work.

She was shakily sipping coffee at her desk when Don buzzed. "I wanted to tell you I picked up a call for you yesterday afternoon. Haven't had a chance to run a message down there."

"Thanks. What was it?"

"It was a hell of a bad connection, so I'm not sure I got it right. I think the operator said—wait a minute. Someone calling on behalf of Miss, um—would it be Cloud? Calling from Bombay, India. Worst connection I ever had."

Marina could hardly move her lips. "Are you sure?"

"Not at all. I couldn't hear. I kept yelling at the operator to spell it, but she just kept saying something like Cloud. Was it important?"

"I don't—I don't know what to say."

"God, Marina, you sound like you're in shock. If I blew something important, I'm really sorry."

"No. No. Did she leave a number?"

"Not that I could hear. I don't think she tried. In fact, the call kind of got cut off. One minute it's all this static and a tiny voice saying 'Cloud,' the next minute nothing."

"She asked for me?"

"I thought so. That's what I understood. That, Bombay, and Cloud. Is it bad news? You sound awful."

"It's OK. Really."

Marina put down the phone. Of course Catherine wouldn't let me off the hook with one letter. She and Nagarajan between them. She writes and calls, he comes into my apartment—but listen, he wasn't there. It was that spicy smell of his. That's how I knew.

It was Jack Sondergard, not Nagarajan, but Jack's smell wasn't the same at all. It was soapier, with lime in it somewhere. In India, she had drunk fresh lime juice mixed with soda water. The thought of its tartness made her nose prickle.

The woman at the telephone company said that even though it was an emergency the call would be very difficult to trace. Her tone of voice said it was probably impossible. Marina left her name and number and hung up.

She couldn't sit here. She paced her office. Catherine and Nagarajan had died years ago. Marina had to figure out—she had to figure out what caused the Loopy Doop disaster, that's what she had to figure out.

She rushed out of her office and half-ran across the pier to the testing division. When she walked in a young man in a smudged white coat said, "You're late. I thought you'd be storming in yesterday afternoon."

She didn't smile. "What about the tensile test?"

"To tell you the truth, I had a little trouble locating the specimens, but it's almost done. I'm about to load the last one now."

She followed him to the tensile testing machine, an apparatus that looked like two columns with steel crossbars holding grips shaped like metal balls, one upended a few inches above the other. He picked up the specimen, a piece of machined steel about two inches long, from a plastic tray. The specimen was threaded at both ends and very thin in the middle. He screwed one threaded end into the top bell grip, the other into the bottom one.

As he worked Marina studied the graph lying beside the tray. "What do the results look like?"

"Checks out fine so far." He responded absently as he adjusted the specimen.

Why couldn't she breathe? "Fine?"

"It's supposed to be 4140, isn't it?"

"Yes."

"Looks to me like that's exactly what it is."

Before she could stop herself she burst out, "How could it be? The hardness test—"

He turned to her, raising his eyebrows, and she cut herself off. Of course hardness was just a guide. The tensile test was the definitive measure of alloy strength. "Let's see how this one does," she said, and he nodded.

He turned on the motor that would draw the crossbars in opposite directions and pull the specimen apart. If Loopy Doop had been made out of soft steel, that would've explained everything. If the steel checked out, then what? Then Jack couldn't blame Singapore, for one thing. For another, she'd be back to square one.

Watching the thin steel being pulled inexorably to the breaking point, she felt the stretch in her own body.

The specimen snapped in the middle. "There she goes," the technician said. He studied the settings on the computer that controlled the machine and wrote down numbers on the chart. He shrugged. "Looks like 4140 to me."

Oh God. "OK."

"I don't know what hardness results you got, but it should've come in at about thirty-five on Rockwell C."

"I got sixty-five on Rockwell B."

"Jeez, you know what I bet?" A smile flashed across his face. "I bet you had the C penetrator in the hardness tester. It's so easy to screw that up. And then you read the B scale instead of the C scale."

How stupid. How incredibly, unutterably stupid, but it was possible. A sixty-five on the B scale would be right above thirty-five on the C scale. What an idiotic, bush-league mistake. Her face felt scalded. "Maybe so," she said.

"Don't worry. I won't tell Sandy."

She walked back to her office and dropped into her chair. Results of the chemical analysis, which would give her the exact components of the alloy, hadn't come in yet. There was still hope, but not much. She'd wait till she got the word on that before telling Jack. In the meantime, she'd better start thinking about what besides weak steel would cause Loopy Doop's leg to break.

*Who had called?* Miss Cloud in Bombay, her own Cloud Sister. Or somebody else. You could tell the police about harassment. Maybe it was against the law to pretend to be a dead person, to try to call your dead sister—no, she was mixing it up. It wasn't against the law to call your dead sister. It was against the law to call your living sister. If you were dead. She laughed, then clamped her teeth down hard to stop herself. When the feeling subsided, she reached for the Loopy Doop file.

That night, Patrick came over. She started violently when the buzzer for the downstairs door sounded, and stared at the speaker box on the wall, her heart surging. When she answered, would Catherine's voice say it was Cloud Sister? She wouldn't answer. After a minute the buzzer sounded again and she pushed the speaker button. "Yes?"

"It's Patrick."

She pushed the button to let him in and collapsed against the wall in the hallway, waiting for him to get the elevator up to her floor.

When she opened the door to his ring, she was amazed at how familiar and at the same time how alien he looked, in his jeans, running shoes, sweater, and glasses, a copy of his favorite magazine, *The Gramophone*, in one hand and a bottle of wine in the other. "I finished rehearsal early," he said.

"Come in."

"Brought some Gamay Beaujolais." He put the wine on the kitchen table, got the corkscrew out of the drawer, and opened the bottle. She watched the light sift through his straight, silky hair as he bent over his task.

He poured and handed her a glass. "You're wondering why I'm here."

She was almost too numb to care. "Yes."

He looked at her closely. "Are you all right? You look wiped out."

For a second, maybe less, she wanted to tell him everything, to babble it all out like a child and beg him to help her. He would. She knew that. The impulse flashed, exploded, died before she could speak. "I'm fine. Working hard."

He sipped and put his glass down. After a moment's hesitation, he said, "Over the past few weeks, I've been seeing somebody. Her name is Nancy."

A nerve pulsed in Marina's throat. "You have?"

"Yes. On the rebound, I guess you might say. She's very nice. But I didn't come here to try to make you jealous."

"You came because—"

"I came because I can't let you go. I can't let you go, and it isn't fair to her, and I guess I have to hear you tell me one more time that we're finished."

"It must be a serious thing with her, then."

"It could be. Sometime. Not the way things are now. What I'm saying is, if there were any chance with you—"

"I know what you're saying."

Marina refilled their glasses. She could tell Patrick she had had a change of heart. She saw the two of them, surrounded by golden light, receding to a tiny black dot and obliterated in a burst of brightness. "It can't happen, Patrick," she said.

His expression didn't change. "So Catherine and Nagarajan are stronger than I am."

Hearing him speak their names was a physical shock. As if he had invoked them, she felt Catherine and Nagarajan hovering.

*I could tell him. He might understand better if he knew they were still real.* She stared at the floor.

He put his glass down. "I'm off."

She walked him to the door. As he opened it she said, "I'm sorry."

His head bobbed in a quick nod. "Goodbye."

She leaned against the door, listening to his footsteps recede. The bottle of wine sat on the table, along with the two glasses. His copy of *The Gramophone* lay on a chair. She wouldn't call him to give it back to him. She sat down again, poured more wine into his glass, and sipped it slowly.

"Try to think," Marina said.

Don closed his eyes. Marina crumpled and threw away the message to call the phone company. The woman had sounded only slightly regretful when she told Marina they'd done what they could, but they couldn't trace the call.

"It was person-to-person for you. I think the operator said, 'Marina Robinson, please. Miss Cloud calling.' No, wait. She said 'Miss Cloud' after I said you weren't here."

Marina wiped her palms on the front of her skirt. "Maybe she said it was Bombay calling the first time," Don said. He screwed his eyes closed tighter. "Anyway, after that there was even more static on the line, and a lot of clicking. I was yelling about leaving a message, and I couldn't hear her much at all, except at one point I thought she was spelling something for me, because I heard her say something about a comma." His eyes opened. "That's it."

"You have no idea what she was spelling?"

"I wish I did, but no."

She turned away, not wanting him to be able to read in her face her desire to hit him, to batter him until he was bruised and pulpy and would be forced to tell her even if he didn't know. Sandy emerged from his office and gestured to her. "You can come in now."

It was only a routine briefing on Loopy Doop, but she wasn't getting through it very well. She couldn't quite connect her thoughts, explain what she'd been doing. What *had* she been doing? The business about the steel and the tests. She started through the story, feeling that she was carrying a heavy bundle and things kept falling out and she had to stop and pick them up. Like a donkey on a dusty road on a hot day, loaded with—oh, mangoes, say, and first one mango and then another tumbled out of the basket and rolled in the dust—

Sandy's eyes were shadowed. "What about the chemical results?" he said.

"I don't know. I should get them today."

"You're telling me that you thought there was a question of low-strength steel but you've got almost nothing to back you up."

"I guess so."

Sandy leaned back in his chair. "You aren't showing me much, Marina."

Rama. Rama. Rama, not comma. The hotel in Bombay where Catherine had stayed when she first went to India. I wrote her there, at the Hotel Rama. *For you to leave without telling me, taking the money we had agreed was for school, is indefensible. I realize that Nagarajan is your god, your guru, or something, but . . .*

Sandy stopped in the middle of a sentence. "Forgive me if I'm boring you."

"No. I mean, you're not."

"I want to see something solid. I don't have to tell you how important this case is, do I?"

"No." It was the Hotel Rama. She could find out the number, maybe call back.

"—Bobo notwithstanding," Sandy was saying.

"All right." She stood up. She noticed that Sandy was frowning as she left.

An envelope from the lab was lying on her desk. The chemical analysis. It could wait, couldn't it, until after she called international information and got the Rama's number? No, better open it. She sucked in her breath.

The steel was 4140. Chrome, molybdenum. Lower-strength alloys wouldn't have those. She dropped the paper on the desk. It had looked so good, so perfect, all because she'd made a mistake on the hardness test and built a theory around it. The whole case was in fragments again. She sat down and reached for the phone, not to call international information but to call Jack Sondergard.

"Oh Jesus, no," he said when she told him.

"I can show you the figures."

"I'm stuck here. Can you bring them over?"

Sondergard's office was in an Embarcadero Center high rise, walking distance from Breakdown. She clutched her portfolio and bent her head against the chilly, wet wind. She didn't want to see Jack. She didn't want to think about it—about him, with his long, pale limbs, his soapy lime smell.

On the Embarcadero Plaza, despite the wind and overcast sky, stands were set up to sell T-shirts, ceramic pots, decorated mirrors, lithographs of San Francisco, to appeal to whatever tourists might venture out. In India, tourists would be surrounded by hawkers selling toys—articulated wooden snakes, serious-looking whips made of braided leather thongs, jointed wire puzzles that could be bent in many shapes. Little-boy peddlers demonstrated the puzzles, going through their singsong "Is ball, is lotus, is bowl, is water jar—" In India there would be a cobra, its hood flared open, swaying to the disturbing music its charmer played.

Sondergard's office had a view of the Golden Gate Bridge rearing into the fog above gray-green swells topped with foam. He closed the door behind her and slid his hand across her back. She shivered from attraction or revulsion.

She didn't look at him as she took the test results from her portfolio, and barely glanced up as she exclaimed that these were definitive, much more so than the hardness test, and that she'd probably blown the hardness test anyway.

He listened, his fingertips placed lightly together, gazing at the papers. When she finished he said, "I was so sure."

"So was I. It had the right feel about it, somehow." As soon as she said the words she was engulfed by grief. As it rushed over her she clung to the tiny voice of rationality that said, You've had theories shot down before. What is this? Then the voice was silenced in the overwhelming conviction that everything was lost, everything, finished, no good. She wanted to say something about how she'd keep trying, but she couldn't say it.

His fingers were under her chin, raising her face to his.

His eyes had a gold glint that she hadn't remembered. "I'd like to come to see you again," he said.

She still couldn't speak. For a long moment she stared at him, feeling herself stretched more and more taut. When it was almost unbearable he let her go. "I'll be in touch," he said.

When she got home that afternoon and opened her mailbox the feeling of the onionskin envelope in her fingers was entirely expected. She carried the letter upstairs. Bombay postmark again, everything the same.

> *Rain Sister,*
> *The* Rig Veda *says, "Now, Agni, quench and revive the very one you have burnt up." Do you understand, Rain Sister?*
>
> *Cloud Sister*

She sat on the edge of her bed. She knew the *Rig Veda* was a collection of Hindu holy texts. From the smattering of information she had picked up during her days with Catherine she remembered that Agni was the god of fire. If Agni was fire, Catherine was the one who had been burnt up, whom the fire must quench and revive. Catherine quenched, revived. Catherine had walked out of the fire that had been kerosene-fed by a mob, leaving her ring behind. Her ring and her bones and her teeth. Reconstituted now, like instant soup, sitting in a hotel room in Bombay tapping out notes and making phone calls.

Marina rested her arms on her knees, bent, and buried her head in them. For a long time, she didn't think at all.

When she raised her head, she knew she was going back to India.

A stewardess in a flowered sari held out a plastic tray, offering wrapped candies scattered around a bowl of anise seeds. Marina shook her head. The plane was full, and around her people were settling into their seats— black-haired women wearing sweaters over saris, post-hippie hippies with long hair and embroidered shirts, an old man in a white cotton coat and a Gandhi cap, Western tourists with cameras, Sikhs in turbans, their beards bound in nets. The fretting of babies counterpointed the pretakeoff babble.

She closed her eyes. She hadn't realized it would be this bad. From the time of her decision until now, she had functioned with all the confidence that had deserted her in the previous days. She had been firm, implacable. Now, chills raked her, and she pulled the thin airline blanket around her chin and tried to push herself deeper into her seat.

She had been prepared for argument from Sandy, but he had seemed almost relieved to let her go. He had made the objection she expected—that it was a wild-goose chase—but without vigor. Of the letters and phone call he had said, "You know this is some nut who read about you in the papers over there and remembers you were involved in the Palika Road incident."

"Some nut who knows the games I used to play with my sister."

"Oh, come on. Maybe it's somebody who knew your sister."

70

"Maybe it's my sister." When she said the words she was embarrassed, as if she'd involuntarily screamed an obscenity.

He shook his head. "I wouldn't go too far with that one." After a moment he punched a button on his intercom. "Hey Don. Marina's going to be taking some vacation time, effective immediately. She'll come out and tell you so you can revise the schedule." He looked at her. "OK?"

"One more thing. Would you tell Jack Sondergard?"

His expression altered slightly, and she wondered whether he and Sondergard had talked about her, laughed about her. "I'll smooth it over. Say it's a family emergency or something," he said.

"Thanks."

"I won't tell Bobo, though. That one's your baby."

In fact, Bobo hadn't seemed to care. She had found him in his solarium, smoking a cigar and clipping an article out of *The Wall Street Journal*. He looked healthier and more tuned in than she'd ever seen him, and she realized that the shock of the Loopy Doop collapse must be wearing off. His manner was brusque, with a touch of the antagonism that had puzzled her before.

"Whatever's right," he said when she told him, turning his cigar between knobby fingers and thumb.

"I'm sure the investigation will be in good hands."

"Yeah. Lots of fine people over at your place, I expect."

Feeling once again rebuffed and confused, she had said goodbye and left him in his cloud of smoke reaching for the telephone.

So here she was, shuffled out the door by her boss and her champion, having made a mess of and then deserted her big case, going back to a place she'd never wanted to see again to look for a dead woman.

She opened her eyes. The announcement about fastening seat belts had started. As she pulled hers tighter, her toe touched her khaki-colored canvas shoulder bag, stowed under the seat in front of her. Without knowing quite why, she had outfitted herself with something almost like a Breakdown "doctor bag." In its zippered compartments were a tape measure, dial calipers, screwdriver, fountain-pen sized flashlight, tweezers, Swiss Army knife, and the pocket-sized camera and flash she liked. Putting the kit together had made her feel that what she was doing might be rational.

Which it wasn't, as every nerve in her body was telling her. The plane began to accelerate. She wished desperately, feverishly, with all her strength that she could get out, go back. Then she grasped the arms of her seat hard as the plane rose.


As the plane droned through the hours from San Francisco to New York, New York to London, Marina dozed and woke, gazed blearily at the screen where movies ran soundlessly, ate and drank at times that had no relationship to her body's messages.

She thought about Loopy Doop. Her mind, perversely, didn't want to let it go. Steel gondolas and aluminum gondolas. Sixty-five Rockwell B and thirty-five Rockwell C. Gonzales Manufacturing and Singapore Metal Works. The little quad case, Tommy or Ronnie.

Think about something else, for God's sake. A picture of Patrick came into her mind. Patrick and Nancy. She saw Patrick caressing Nancy, his hands light and tender and warm, his breath blowing the hair next to Nancy's ear as he whispered to her. She didn't know what color Nancy's hair was. She closed her eyes and tried to sleep again.

When the plane took off from London for Bombay, she was fully awake, with a film of sweat on her body that came not from heat but from fear. She remembered the other time she'd made this trip. Then, she had been rigid with determination, coming to get her sister and take her home. She had seen Nagarajan herself by that time, and knew what she was up against.

Catherine had been simmering with excitement for weeks before Nagarajan's visit to San Francisco. She began wearing a sari. She stood on street corners with it streaming in the wind, handing out leaflets announcing his appearance.

"Aren't you cold?" Marina asked one morning as Catherine was leaving the house with her stack of flyers. Catherine, who by that time seemed to regard anything Marina said as a criticism, didn't reply. Marina stretched out her hand. "Can I see one of those?" Catherine handed one over and left. In the brief moment when the sheet changed hands, Marina saw goose pimples on Catherine's arm.

She studied the leaflet. There was a picture on it, a black-and-white version of the one in Catherine's room, and the words, "SRI NAGARAJAN WILL VISIT US! The master of the wisdom of the cobra shares his knowledge at Bay Area appearances." There was a list of dates and times. She decided to go see him.

On the evening she chose, she waited outside the auditorium hoping to slip in without Catherine's noticing her. As she paced nervously, a voice spoke from the shadows at the side of the building. "You wonder whether to see me, is it?" the voice said. The voice had a musical lilt and the suggestion of a British accent. "Is it?" the voice persisted, and when she realized it was addressing her, she saw him.

He stood half-hidden in a dim angle of the building. He wore a dark robe, and his face seemed to float disembodied between it and his mass of black hair. He laughed, and she saw his eyes glimmer as they caught the light when he tilted his head. "Come here," he said.

As she approached, he placed his palms together and bent his head over them. "*Namaste*, I greet you," he said. She could not guess his age. In the indirect light his face looked completely unlined. The one thing that was different from the retouched photograph was a mottled, puckered scar, a bit larger than a quarter, on his neck near his collarbone.

"Before I speak, I always stand out to watch," he said. "I see the people who rush in, eager for what I may offer. Their faces cast a pale light—the light of need. Other faces cast other lights. Often I see the wavering light of fear. On yours"—he peered at her—"on yours, I think I see the harsh light of doubt." His smile broadened. "Am I correct?"

"You're correct."

He clapped his hands, seeming delighted. "You see, I read these faces very well. I must, to see what they are bringing me. Then I will know what to return to them."

Marina tried to marshal her thoughts. Could s.
him about Catherine, get him to loosen his hold? "My
sister—" she began.

He went on as if she hadn't spoken. "People bring me
what they are looking for, and what they find in me is
what they have brought. That is a paradox, do you think?
But true all the same."

"Why do people—my sister—give themselves up—"

"It is what I have said. They come to fill their lack
with me. They find in me what they already have, yet it
seems to come from me." He laughed again. "It amuses
me very much."

"For them it's serious."

"To be serious is their need. Am I myself serious?
That is another question."

"You mean this is all a sham? A trick?"

He shook his head vigorously. A faint, pleasant, spicy
smell wafted to her. "Dear lady, you have not understood. I am Nagarajan, the king of the cobras, the
dweller in the deep well, the keeper of the great
treasure."

"You just said—"

"I said perhaps I am not serious. But I am Nagarajan." He cocked his head to one side. "It puzzles you?
You will come, you will understand." He put his palms
together and bowed again, then turned and walked
swiftly away from her and disappeared through a door in
the side of the building.

What had she expected? Marina wondered as she
watched him go. A fanatic, harsh and humorless. Not
that trace of mockery, that undeniable attractiveness.

She stood in the back of the auditorium. It was not
full. The Bay Area had had quite a dose of the wisdom of

the East already, and Nagarajan was an unknown newcomer. In front of the curtain, softly lit, was a low divanlike structure furnished with pillows, a gold-painted cobra umbrella fanning out above it. In front of the divan was a microphone. Indian music, complex and sinuous, played softly.

An American wearing white trousers and a knee-length shirt with loose sleeves came out and began to lead the crowd in a singsong chant: *Guru Nagarajan, Parama Sukhadam. Guru Nagarajan, Chrana Shranam.*

The crowd had begun tremulously, but the sound grew in volume and confidence as more voices joined in. Marina could still reproduce the chant in her head without even stopping to think about it. Guru Nagarajan, Eternal giver of happiness. Guru Nagarajan, We take refuge at his feet. The auditorium resounded, vibrated. At the height of it, the light that had been trained on the divan went out and, when it came back up, brighter and whiter than it had been, Nagarajan was seated under-neath the cobra umbrella. There was a collective catch-ing of breath, and Marina felt her own throat open and close. Then the audience broke into wave after wave of applause.

Marina remembered little of what Nagarajan had said that evening. The message was not in the words, but in the modulations, the gestures, the projection of wisdom accompanied by an undercurrent suggesting strange and infinite possibilities.

"You tell me the world is full of pain," Nagarajan said, "and I tell you pain is a veil. Suffering is a veil. We must pierce it, we must pass through it, we must leave it. We feel that we carry burdens, without knowing that our burdens are ourselves. What we carry is not separate

76

from us, but we are our own burdens. We must leave ourselves behind." Although he did not use his smooth, distinct voice theatrically, it seemed to tremble with harnessed power. Marina kept reminding herself that what he was saying was standard mystical fare, yet she felt intently focused on every word.

When he finished, the applause was frenzied. Marina was exhausted. A white-haired woman near her was weeping silently. Nagarajan continued to sit beneath the cobra umbrella, and the crowd moved down the aisles toward him.

From her place in the back she could see Catherine, in her sari, hovering near him with a little knot of other Westerners in Indian clothing. She was too far away for Marina to see her face clearly, but Marina could guess that it was alive with joy. She turned and left the auditorium.

Marina was not surprised when, a few days later, Catherine told her she wanted to return to India with Nagarajan.

"Absolutely not. Not until you finish school."

Catherine twisted an end of her sari around her finger. "You don't understand."

"I do. I went to one of his talks."

Catherine's eyes widened. "You did? Then you can see—"

"I can see that he's extremely good at manipulating crowds. I can't see that you should go to India with him."

"He's starting an ashram near Bombay. I'd be in at the beginning."

"What's he using to finance this ashram? Don't tell me. Contributions from his disciples."

"What if he is?"

"We have enough money for you to finish college. We can't use it to finance somebody's ashram."

"I don't care about college."

"Catherine, no is no."

So, as Marina supposed she had known she would, Catherine took the money and left anyway. And Marina, full of rage at being deserted and fear of Nagarajan and his power, went after her.

Then, she had been full of conviction. Now, she was convinced of nothing. The request to buckle seat belts came over the loudspeaker. She brought the back of her seat upright and prepared for landing.

# India

MARINA DESCENDED THE STEPS OF THE AIRplane into the heat of the Bombay night. She waited on the tarmac with the other passengers for the bus to the terminal, wondering how she could ever have forgotten what the air was like: the omnipresent faint smell of spices, smoke from outdoor cooking fires, the suggestion of salt water. Her jacket, which had been inadequate against San Francisco's foggy chill, was too heavy now. She took it off and rolled up the sleeves of her blouse.

The dingy hall where she had her passport stamped, cleared customs, and changed money was filled with chatter and confusion. She moved from place to place in a daze of weariness, shoving forward whatever document was required. Finally, her suitcase reclaimed, she straggled with her fellow passengers through glass doors into a maelstrom of dark, eager, searching faces and outstretched hands. "Baksheesh, madam. No mama, no

papa, no money." "Postcard, madam? Look. Very
beautiful." "Madam, you have hotel? You want good
hotel? I take you, madam?"

She had made no arrangements, but had never doubted
where she would stay. "Yes, yes, I have a hotel." She
gave her suitcase to one of the several porters vying for
her attention. "Taxi."

He moved off at a jog trot, and Marina hurried after
him to a line of taxis, yellow with black tops, and
smaller, open-sided minicabs with fringed roofs. She
paid the porter, and when the turbaned, beak-nosed
driver turned to her she said, "Hotal Rama."

Obviously, she must stay at the Rama, the hotel where
Catherine had stayed, the hotel the phone call came
from. The cab careened through the night, passing
minicabs, people on bicycles, decorated trucks, bullock
carts. As they neared the city, the roadside was built up
with lean-tos of canvas or woven screens housing
families of squatters. Shadowy figures crouched near
small fires.

Soon, the sea smell was stronger, mixed with a hint of
sewage. Huge billboards advertising films loomed over
the streets. They passed Haji Ali's mosque, which in the
dark seemed to float on the ocean like a minareted boat.
When the car stopped at a traffic light a leprous child
pressed his face to Marina's window, holding up stump-
fingered hands: "No mama, no papa—" The driver
spoke sharply, and the child drifted back into the night as
the light changed.

Now they were passing Chowpatty Beach, its or-
angish-gold sand and the trees growing out of it luridly
illuminated by electric bulbs strung overhead, its *bhel
puri* stalls as busy as if it were noon. When they reached

80

Marine Drive, with its curving line of posh hotels, towers of glass overlooking the seawall, the driver turned inland into a warren of streets and she lost all clue as to where she was.

They wound slowly down a narrow, badly illuminated street. In open-fronted shops men smoked cigarettes and talked. Next to a food stand with sweetmeats piled in conical mounds a vendor squatted on the sidewalk with his tray of *beedis*, loose cigarettes. The driver stopped in front of a building with latticed porches on the upper floors. An electric bulb illuminated a signboard on which was painted "Hotel Rama." Beneath the sign, the front door stood open. Along with the faint light that shone from it came the piercing voice of a woman singing what might have been a highly charged lament. Marina paid the driver and carried her suitcase inside.

The sound was even louder in the lobby, which was furnished only with a greasy-looking blue sofa and a straight-backed chair sprung in the seat. A poster advertising Elephanta Island and its cave temple curled from the wall. A brown plastic radio, the source of the singing, sat on the check-in desk. Behind the desk leaned a sleepy-looking young man wearing a short-sleeved polyester shirt printed with a colorful design. Marina immediately noticed the antiquated-looking telephone switchboard. That was where the call had come from.

She approached the desk. "I'd like a room."

The man yawned and turned the radio down a fraction. "You have reservation?"

"No, I don't."

He leafed slowly through the yellowing pages of the registration book. "You wish to stay how long?"

"I'm not sure. Several days, probably."

He sucked his breath in through his teeth, still turning pages. Marina leaned wearily against the desk. She had no doubt there was a room, and also no doubt that he must finish his routine before he gave it to her. "Let me see, let me see." He ran a finger down a page. "Yes. Number eleven is free."

She signed the register, the wail of the radio cutting into her brain. She thought vaguely that she might start her inquiries now, but dismissed the idea. The desk clerk hit a bell, and a bent old man emerged from somewhere and picked up her suitcase. She followed him up a flight of creaking stairs and down a gloomy hall that smelled of dust with a strong overlay of insecticide. The sound of the radio had receded only slightly by the time they reached the door marked eleven.

The lobby had given her an idea of what to expect. A narrow iron bed, sagging in the middle, stood in a corner, its thin pad of a mattress covered with a thread-bare blanket. A dressing table listed on spindly legs under a cloudy mirror. The room was lit by a bare bulb hanging from the ceiling. Wires protruded from the socket intended for a twin bulb. The porter put down the suitcase and turned on the light in the bathroom. She glanced in for a ritual inspection. A rust-stained sink, a toilet, an open shower with no curtain or stall, a red plastic pail and dipper for those who preferred to bathe Indian style. A cigarette butt floated in the toilet bowl. "Fine," she said. She tipped him and he left, murmuring, "Memsa'ab."

She undressed, stood under the tepid trickle of the shower, dragged her nightgown from her suitcase and put it on. The bed gave a raspy twang as she crawled in. The radio was still playing what seemed to be the same song when she fell asleep.

The next morning the radio was silent. Sunlight slanted through the lobby, catching motes of spinning dust. Although Marina could smell something frying, and occasional clatters and raised voices indicated that the hotel was not completely deserted, the lobby was empty. She studied the Elephanta poster for a few moments, then wandered to the desk. The registration book lay on the counter where it had been the night before. She reached out and let her fingers rest on its cracked black cover. Still nobody. Why not? She slid the book around so it faced her, glanced over her shoulder, and opened it.

It didn't surprise her to discover that the Hotel Rama's bookkeeping system seemed haphazard. It was difficult to tell, though, because many of the guests had signed the register in Indian languages, or what she guessed were Indian languages. Only occasionally was something written in English. The Miss Cloud call had been made on January fifteenth. Here was January. Even if I can find January fifteenth, that'll only tell me who checked in on that day. The person who made the call could have been here a week beforehand. Could even live here.

Suppose it was Catherine. She might walk in now; this minute I could see her. She might have been badly burned, be terribly scarred, wear a veil over her face to hide it. It could be she doesn't want to show herself to me because of that, and that's why she's been so mysterious.

This must be January fifteenth. She stared at the scribbled, wavering lines, at least half of them written in characters she couldn't begin to decipher. Somebody could decipher them, though. *If I had a copy and a little time.* She raised her head and looked around again, her hand at the same time going into her canvas bag and closing around the hard plastic case of her little camera.

It took her only seconds to move the book into better light and shoot the pages she wanted. As she closed the book and readjusted it in its former position she heard a sound. Peering at her from a doorway on the other side of the desk was a bent old woman with sunken cheeks and gray hair.

Marina couldn't control a start of surprise, but she got hold of herself and said, "Can you help me? I'm looking for someone who can help me."

The old woman disappeared. As Marina wondered whether to wait or not, a heavily pregnant woman in a red sari, her blue-black hair braided down her back, entered through the same doorway. "Madam?" she said.

Surely the old woman hadn't had time to say she'd seen Marina photographing the registration book—if she had seen. *Act businesslike.* "I'm looking for someone who telephoned me in the United States. The call came from this hotel. The message wasn't clear, unfortunately, and it was important. Can you help me?"

The woman said, "Telephone?"

Her English, Marina realized, was limited. "Telephone."

"No telephone now."

"No, I don't want to make a call. I want to know—"

"You see Raki. Telephone."

"Raki? Where is Raki?"

"Not here. Later."

"How much later? When?"

"Later. See Raki. Telephone." The woman inclined her head with an air of finality and left the room.

There seemed to be no choice but to see Raki later. She was hungry. Despite the pervasive cooking smell the Rama seemed to lack any sort of restaurant or dining room for guests. She walked outside to get her bearings.

The sunlight was hot and brilliant in the shabby street. Near the sweetmeat stand two boys crouched on the sidewalk tinkering with an ancient motorcycle. The *beedi* vendor squatted near a huge film billboard depicting a buxom, sari-clad woman with a huge tear on one cheek, and, behind her, a handsome man staring at her with a yearning expression. A wooden cart pulled by two bullocks, bells clinking around their necks, made its laborious way through the cars, bicycles, and minicabs that crowded the street. Two men passed by, carrying stacks of wicker cages in which green birds fluttered. Under the billboard was a small establishment whose sign proclaimed it to be the Kumkum Cafe. Maybe she could get breakfast there.

She could. She bought the *Times of India* and read it while she ate chapaties and vegetable curry that made her mouth tingle. A government scandal was brewing; a woman had been doused with kerosene and set on fire by her husband's family because her dowry wasn't large enough; a dacoit, or bandit, who claimed to be India's modern Robin Hood, was terrorizing villages south of Bombay; a follower of Gandhi had died. Putting the paper aside, she sat over a last cup of tea and planned her next move. She should visit the consulate, in case they knew something that could help. They wouldn't welcome her, but they never had. She paid her bill and went to look for a taxi.

I can't do it. I can't go in there again. As the taxi moved away from her, she shaded her eyes against the glare of the sun reflected off the consulate's white walls. A line of Indians waiting for something, probably a turn at the visa office, straggled down the block.

The building had been a maharajah's palace. She remembered how overwhelmed she had been at age twenty-two, climbing the steps practically on tiptoe, creeping along the corridors, an unwanted, bothersome supplicant. I won't. It's too much.

Her legs felt like overstretched elastic. They would never carry her up those steps into a past she would do anything to avoid. Maybe if I lean forward almost far enough to fall, I'll move. She moved. She started to climb.

The office to which she was eventually shown had half-closed blinds and a ceiling fan, but the man behind the desk was not Mr. Hayes. Marina wondered where Mr. Hayes had been posted. Maybe he had retired. She remembered sitting in a hotel room with an anguished little group of Americans, survivors of the other two disciples who had died, while he explained the details of the U.S. government's protest. He read the text of the message and said, "We're vigorously pursuing the investigation, but in a case of mob violence it's almost impossible to isolate the guilty parties. Few Indians will talk at all, and those who will say either the crowd was after Nagarajan and didn't realize he was in jail, or they thought the ashram was empty after his arrest and were burning it in symbolic protest."

He stubbed out a cigarette. A woman was weeping

against the shoulder of her tight-lipped husband. "Those are all rationalizations after the fact, pseudoexplanations for what was basically an irrational act," Mr. Hayes said.

"My son is dead, and you talk to me about irrational acts. It was murder," the man said. He and his wife had later brought suit, charging that the investigation had been mishandled. Marina had gotten a letter asking if she wanted to join them. She hadn't answered.

Marina's last memory of Mr. Hayes was of his seeing her off. She hadn't expected it, and was surprised to see him at the airport, a nondescript little figure in his usual white short-sleeved shirt and tightly knotted tie. They had waited for her boarding call. When it came, he shook her hand and said, "I'm sorry, Miss Robinson. We were too late."

"None of it was your fault."

As she walked toward the plane she turned once and looked back. When he saw her looking, he waved. She had waved back and turned to leave India, as she thought, forever.

This James Curtis did not look like Mr. Hayes. He was plump and fortyish, with reddish-blond hair and beard and a floral tie loosened at the neck of his pink candy-striped shirt. What he had in common with Mr. Hayes was an air of being harassed. "I don't know about letting you in the files," he was saying. "I'd have to check with some people."

The close air in the office was made closer by the smoke from his pipe, which he puffed steadily while looking at the letters from Cloud Sister.

"I thought the files might tell me something helpful."

"Yes, so you said." Mr. Curtis placed his still-smoking pipe in an ashtray. "You didn't say helpful with what, exactly."

"I'm not sure. I don't know what I'd be looking for. I do know that either my sister is alive or somebody wants me to think she is. You understand that I'd like to find out more."

"Yes. I understand. And yet— Let me try to explain our point of view." He picked the pipe up again, toying with the bowl. "I was fairly new in the service when the Palika Road incident occurred. I can tell you that it is still considered the textbook case of the worst possible peacetime civilian incident. People cringe when it's mentioned. You see what I'm driving at?"

"Not exactly."

"What I'm driving at is, nobody wants it stirred up again. We don't, the Indians don't. You come over here with absolutely no warning, go through the files, ask questions. Pretty soon, all the old wounds start to bleed again. Would you like to see that happen?"

"You're forgetting that I was perfectly willing to let it alone. It wouldn't let *me* alone."

"You said it yourself. Some crank saw your name in the paper."

"A crank who knows details of my personal history."

Mr. Curtis sighed. "Let's have some coffee."

When the steaming cups had been served, he scratched his beard and said, "I don't suppose you'd want to take my advice."

"Not if it's to go home."

"It is."

"Then no."

"We can't have you running around the countryside asking about Palika Road. We just can't have it."

Time to take the gloves off. "Forgive me for putting it this way, but is there anything you can do to stop me? I mean, without causing some of the trouble you're so anxious to avoid?"

He looked at her keenly over the top of his cup. Finally he said, "If I let you look in the file, will you promise not to make me sorry?"

"I promise not to make you sorry deliberately."

"OK. Follow me."

It was hot in the file room, despite a rattling air conditioner. Perspiration trickled through Marina's hair as she sat at the wooden table with stacks of documents in front of her. Here was the police report of Nagarajan's suicide. The guard testified, "When I made my round at eight o'clock in the evening, he was sitting on his bed mat with his head on his knees. When I returned at nine o'clock, he was hanging from the bars of his cell. Around his neck was a noose he had made from strips of his clothing." An attached page noted that Nagarajan had been cremated the same night.

Dizzy with jet lag and bad memories, she picked up another sheaf of papers. This was the dossier about the riot and fire on Palika Road. The few witnesses whose testimony was recorded had avoided specifics. The story of a tenant farmer was typical:

We were drinking tea at the shop of Govinda when two men came in. I do not know their names. They were talking about the evil that was done to Agit More. They said this evil had polluted Halapur. We heard voices outside and went to see, and there were people with rocks and sticks, talking of the evil at the ashram. Someone said, "Yes, yes, we must go there."

As we went along, other joined us. I wanted to go away, but I was afraid. When it started to burn, I ran away. I didn't see.

The accounts were confused and fragmentary. Nobody knew the whole story, and because all the principles were dead there had been no trial. The people who had gone through the burned-out ashram had thought they found the remains of three bodies, but couldn't they have been mistaken? Such mistakes had been made before. Her head was throbbing.

Before she left, she stopped to thank Mr. Curtis. He nodded. "What do you plan to do now?"

"I don't know. I have a couple of leads to follow up. Then, I don't know."

"Let me ask you again, formally, not to pursue this."

"All right, you've asked."

"Let me warn you, formally, that you can get into a lot of trouble and cause yourself and us embarrassment."

"OK. I understand."

"Let me formally dissociate myself and the consulate from whatever you undertake in the matter of Palika Road."

"Fine."

"One final request. Would you leave your home and Bombay addresses with the secretary for our files?" He stood to see her out.

Marina returned to the Rama. The lobby was as deserted as before, and she couldn't summon the strength to inquire about Raki. She felt almost sick from the effort of going to the consulate, reading the files, dragging herself through it all again. She fell on her creaking bed and slept.

She was awakened at dusk by a tap on the door. After splashing water on her face she answered. Standing there was a slim young Indian man. He wore a beautifully tailored blue suit, a starched white shirt, a rep tie. His short hair was brushed neatly back, and he wore black-rimmed glasses and carried a briefcase. "My name is Vijay Pandit," he said. "Mr. Curtis sent me to help you."

Marina bit into her *samosa*, chewed, and felt her mouth begin to burn. She took a large swallow of beer. "So Mr. Curtis sent you to be my keeper," she said.

Vijay Pandit was chewing an *idli*. Except for a table of men drinking tea in a corner, the two of them were the sole patrons of the Kumkum Cafe. "A helper only," he said.

Marina had checked his identification, which said he worked for the United States Information Agency. Not satisfied with the card that looked perfectly in order, she called James Curtis's office to make sure they had heard of this very proper-looking young man. A secretary confirmed that Vijay Pandit, who worked for USIA, was on temporary assignment to Mr. Curtis. Through all this Vijay Pandit stood patiently in the hall, obviously unwilling to cross the threshold of her room. When she handed his card back he said, "Shall we discuss over tiffin?"

Her mouth was anesthetized by now, and she was able

to continue eating. "I don't understand. Mr. Curtis made a point of dissociating himself formally from anything I plan to do."

"Yes. Formally, I am not here."

Marina thought Mr. Curtis had a hell of a nerve. She should have realized at the consulate that he was letting her go too easily. Now he had saddled her with a prim, toe-the-line civil servant who would be a direct pipeline on her every move. She studied Vijay Pandit, who was the picture of a company man, with his exquisite manners, his neat grooming, his sincerity. Having him around would be like having a ball and chain on her leg.

He looked up, noticed her examining him, and smiled, tentatively. She looked away. She could get rid of him. If she simply told him to go away, what could he do? He couldn't force himself on her.

"You would like something else? More beer?" he said.

"No thanks." She pushed her plate away and turned to him. "What's you assignment, exactly?"

"Simply to aid you in your inquiries." He smiled again, more broadly. "And, as you have probably guessed, to be in touch with the consulate immediately if you get into trouble."

At least he was honest about it. A thought occurred to her. "What languages do you speak?"

"English, as you already know. Also Marathi, the language of Maharashtra, the state we are in. Also Hindi, our other national language besides English. I studied a bit of French at university, but I don't really speak."

"You read those too?"

"Yes."

He would probably have no trouble reading the pages

she had photographed from the hotel register. Having admitted one advantage to having him around, she thought of others. He knew the territory. He would probably have access to a car and driver. If he got to be a problem, she could always ditch him later. "Maybe I should tell you what I'm doing, Mr. Pandit," she said.

"Please. You will call me Vijay," he said, and leaned forward.

She started with Catherine and ended with photographing the register and being surprised by the old woman. By the time she finished talking, the cafe was full, and bright lights illuminated the smoky interior.

Vijay listened closely, interrupting only a few times with questions. He sat back. "So you must speak with this Raki," he said.

"Yes, but he doesn't seem to be around very much."

"Shall we go now? Perhaps he has returned."

The lobby of the Rama was more alive than Marina had ever seen it. Two men in loud print shirts conversed rapidly by the door. A massively fat man sat on the couch, pudgy hands resting on his knees. The old woman she had seen earlier stood half-hidden in a doorway. At the switchboard sat a small, dark, misshapen man whom she knew must be Raki.

He climbed laboriously from the stool he was sitting on and walked to the registration desk with a limping, scraping gait. His chin barely cleared the top of the desk. His face was mobile and alive with intelligence, and despite his twisted body his arms and chest were full and muscular. When she asked about the January fifteenth call he tilted his head to one side. "A call to the States? That would have been very expensive call, madam."

"I guess it would. So do you—"

"For such a thing we would have required guarantee of payment. We are small hotel, Indian hotel. Not like larger, Western-style hotels, where such calls are made on daily, even hourly, basis."

"I know. That's why I was hoping you'd—"

"But madam, for that I must check my records."

"You mean you can't remember?"

Raki's eyes widened. "So much goes on. Every day, every day. I will look in the records."

The registration book, Marina noticed, was no longer on the counter. Raki spoke in another language to the old woman, who went down the hall. She returned in a few minutes, clutching the book. As she gave it to him, she darted a look at Marina.

Raki climbed on a chair behind the counter, deposited the book on the desk, and bent over it. "It is January you were saying?"

"The fifteenth."

He opened the book, leafed through, then hesitated. "The pages are gone."

Marina was so surprised she couldn't react for a moment. The old woman, she saw, had moved into the lobby and was standing near Vijay. "Gone?"

"Someone has pulled them out. You can see."

Raki pushed the book toward her and she saw the uneven edges where several pages had been ripped out. "How could it have happened?" she said.

Raki didn't seem upset or perplexed. "They tear them out sometimes, use them to start the fires," he said blandly. "I tell them not to do it, but they are ignorant." He spoke to the old woman, a sharp tone in his voice, and she left the room.

"Does this mean you can't remember the call, and you don't know who made it?"

His eyes were limpid and sincere. "So many things, madam. So many things. Now the pages are missing. I cannot say."

Marina turned away, and Vijay said in her ear, "It is too bad. Shall we go drink some tea?"

As they emerged on the sidewalk Marina said, "He didn't even bother to think up a plausible story. He knows who tore those pages out, and why."

"I expect you are right," Vijay said, glancing up and down the street. "Lucky you have your photographs."

Marina gnawed her knuckle. "Those torn-out pages mean there's something to hide. Don't you think?"

"Possibly. There may be other explanations."

Marina realized they were standing once more in front of the Kumkum Cafe. "I don't reallly want any tea."

"Nor do I." Vijay sounded amused. "But I think we had better have some anyway. I think we must wait a little, to see what will happen."

As they sipped their tea, Vijay kept glancing toward the street. "What are you looking for?" Marina asked.

"I'm not sure, but I think—yes, I am right. There she is."

Marina followed his nod and saw, across the jammed, noisy street, the old woman from the hotel standing in the mouth of an alley. Vijay stood up. "Let's go quickly."

The old woman drew them farther down the alley, speaking rapidly and breathily to Vijay. He answered, then turned to Marina. "She says she can tell you what you want to know about the telephone call. She also says her daughter is very sick. That means we must offer to pay something. We shall say it is for medicine.''

"Of course."

A low-voiced flurry of conversation followed. Then Vijay said, "I have told her we will give her twenty-five rupees now. If she gives good information, we will give her another twenty-five.''

"Some bribe. Not even five dollars."

"For her it is a great deal. All right?"

"Sure." Marina dug in her bag.

When the money had disappeared somewhere in the folds of the woman's sari, she spoke again to Vijay. He interrupted a few times. When she stopped speaking, he said, "She doesn't know much. She says someone did make a call to the U.S. It was a man, she doesn't know his name. There was discussion about paying for the call. Although the man paid for the call and for his room also, he left the same day and didn't stay the night.''

The old woman watched Marina anxiously during this explanation, her head bobbing up and down.

Marina's mouth was dry. "She says a man made the call. Ask her if she's seen a—a woman. A Western woman with yellow hair, who wears a sari." Or is terribly scarred and wears a veil. Or who has dyed her hair red and wears blue jeans, or Paris gowns. As she listened to their exchange she realized she wasn't breathing.

"She doesn't remember such a woman," Vijay said at last.

Wilting, she asked, "Does she have anything else to say?"

"One thing. Raki tore the pages out of the book

himself. She saw him do it, and hide them in a tin trunk in the office where he keeps papers."

"I thought he'd done it. I wonder why. Is that all?"

Vijay and the woman spoke again, briefly. "That's all."

Marina handed him another twenty-five rupees. "Tell her I hope her daughter gets better."

When the woman had taken the money and scuttled down the alley, Marina said, "How did you know she would come after us?"

"While you were talking with Raki I watched her. I thought I could see that she understood some of what was going on. After she brought the book I walked away in case she wanted to make a sign to me. She did, or I was fairly certain she did."

"Why did she do it?"

"How much money does she make, do you suppose? Perhaps fifty rupees a month, perhaps less. She saw an opportunity. It's even possible her daughter really is sick."

"Did she see me photographing the pages this morning?"

"She didn't say so, and of course I didn't ask her."

They had been walking along the bright, smoky street, elbowing past the knots of people buying food and drink at the open-air stalls. "The next thing is to get my film developed, so we can see what was written on the register," Marina said.

"Yes. In fact"—Vijay consulted the bulky digital watch on his wrist—"a man who does some photographic work for USIA is probably still in his shop. We will tell him it is an emergency."

Until now, it hadn't occurred to Marina that what she was doing could be dangerous. As she and Vijay waited in the stifling cubbyhole that was the photographer's shop, though, her foreboding was as pervasive and strong as the chemical smell. *Raki tore the pages from the register because of me, because I asked about the telephone. Couldn't that mean somebody knows what I'm doing, doesn't want me to do it?*

*Somebody doesn't want me to see Catherine.* She stirred, trying to rid herself of the panic the thought aroused.

"It will not be long now," Vijay said.

"Good." *My ally. An ally who, if I go against his mandate, will turn into a hindrance or even an enemy.*

To keep from thinking, she said, "What do you do when you aren't protecting the consulate from embarrassment?"

"Less interesting things. I try in various ways to smooth interactions between your people and mine. I arrange, I explain. Many difficulties demand the attention of—how is it said?—a minor functionary."

"You grew up in Bombay?"

He seemed pleased to talk. "Yes. My father is a judge of the high court. I live with my parents and my two older brothers and their wives and children. I have two older sisters, too, who are married. I am the youngest."

"Your sisters and their husbands live with you, too?"

"They live with the families of their husbands. It is the Indian custom, you know, for families to stay together. In America, they tell me, families move apart. Which is better? I don't know."

"I live alone."

He seemed shocked. "If you are sick, or need help,, or money, who helps you?"

Patrick's image came briefly into her mind. "I have to take care of myself."

After a moment's silence he said, "My parents are looking for a wife for me."

Marina was shocked in her turn. "You mean you won't have any choice about who you marry?"

"These days many marriages are not arranged. Since I am the youngest, and my parents have grandchildren already, they were in no hurry. I suppose I might have had someone of my own choosing. Now that I am twenty-five, though, they say they have waited long enough. They want to see me settled, with a family."

"How do you feel about it?"

He lifted his shoulders. "All right." Marina thought she saw unhappiness flicker across his smooth, pleasant face.

The photographer emerged from the darkroom holding curling sheets of still-damp paper. Marina took one. The writing looked slightly grainy from being blown up, but it would be legible.

"Now we shall see," said Vijay.

Minutes later, they were in his small office with the photographs spread under the desk light. Vijay circled his forefinger over the prints and selected one. "Here is January fifteenth." He adjusted his glasses.

He leaned back in his chair and rocked gently, staring at the page. A long time seemed to pass. At last he said, "Yes, yes." He beckoned her. "I think I have found it."

The page was a hodgepodge of cramped, wavery lines, items crossed out, arithmetical calculations, and words scribbled in the margin. Looking at the section he indicated, the first thing she noticed was that some of it was in English. Sandwiched between lines in a language she didn't know were the words "Vincent Shah, Delightful Novelty Company," and a Bombay address. Vijay put his finger on the name and said, "I believe this was written by Raki, or someone else at the hotel. It was the same hand in which other notations are made—how many days someone will stay, costs—do you see?"

"Right."

"This"—Vijay pointed to the line above Vincent Shah's name and address—"is another name, Anand Kumar. For profession he has listed commercial traveler, and he has given an address in Ahmedabad. The call, you see here, a hundred and fifty rupees, was charged to Anand Kumar. And then this"—he pointed to the last line—"is also written by Raki." He ran his finger under the line. "I do not know what to make of it. It says, 'I have told the rope with teeth'—or you might say the toothed rope, something like that. I'm not—"

"No," Marina said.

She saw the heavy-lidded eyes, heard the voice in a rhythmic singsong: "I come from the deep well, from the rich kingdom Nagaloka. I am the wind-eater, the cardamom leaf, the conch shell, the oleander flower, the rope with teeth."

The stumbling response came from Catherine and the others: "The wind-eater, the cardamom leaf, the conch shell, the oleander flower, the rope with teeth."

Another time he had said, teasing, "If a serpent bites you, Marina, it is most taboo to say, 'A serpent has bitten me.' You must say instead, 'A rope has touched me.'"

A rope has touched me.

Somebody was talking. She watched Vijay's lips move, but couldn't separate his words from the roaring in her ears. Not another one. What is this, Resurrection Day? Will I walk outside and run into Mother and Dad on the street?

She finally heard, "—matter?"

And in a few moments was able to say, "It's Nagarajan."

"The wind-eater was because of the way a snake's tongue darts in and out," Marina said. "The oleander flower because it's poisonous like snakes are. I forget why the conch shell and the cardamom leaf. I think they had to do with legendary naga kings. The rope with teeth is obvious."

Indian waiters in knee-length red coats, glossy black boots, and elaborate turbans suggestive of regimental uniforms moved among the tables in the bar. Most of the patrons were American or Western European, probably guests at the posh hotel where the bar was located. On a bandstand a combo played a wavering version of "Yesterday."

Marina felt woozy from shock and from the beer she had drunk to combat it. "It's the only explanation."

Vijay toyed with his glass. "I said before. It is an expression only. There is no reason to think it means anything."

"No, no. It's significant. It has to be significant."

"How can you be sure? You have been thinking a great deal about this Nagarajan. You may see something where there is nothing to see."

He was wrong. "It's written there, 'I have told Nagarajan.'"

"Nagarajan died, killed himself in prison."

"That's what they said. Maybe it wasn't true."

Vijay regarded her soberly. She could see he was worried about what he'd gotten into. First she thought her sister hadn't died. Now she was saying Nagarajan might have survived too. She felt as if her life were unfolding into something that, when fully displayed, would look very much like a nightmare. If Nagarajan's alive—I can't think about it. Only, if Nagarajan's alive, he'll know about Catherine. If there's anything I'm sure of, it's that she would never forsake him.

"Can you tell me," said Vijay carefully, "any possible explanation—"

"No. I can only say he sometimes called himself the toothed rope, and the Rama is the hotel he and his followers stayed at before they established the ashram at Halapur. There is a connection. It isn't something out of the blue."

As she spoke she felt more persuaded herself. According to the files at the consulate, the guard had seen Nagarajan hanging in his cell and the body had been cremated the same night. Because of the climate, it was common to dispose of dead bodies quickly. She wondered how many other people had seen the body, or would have known whether or not a body was actually Nagarajan's if they'd seen it. Perhaps all he'd have had to do was bribe one guard. He could have bought his way out. He might even have talked his way out. He could be extremely persuasive.

She remembered arriving at the Halapur ashram for the first time, at the mud-colored house that squatted among other mud-colored houses on Palika Road. Her head had swum from the heat as she paid the minicab driver and stood with her suitcase at the gate. Giggling neighborhood children, Agit More no doubt among them, had gathered to stare as she stood organizing her thoughts. Catherine had come out on the veranda and stood, leaning on the railing, watching her.

Marina had gotten the Halapur address from Nagarajan's followers in San Francisco. She hadn't told Catherine she was coming. When Marina crossed the bare earth and climbed the veranda steps she saw that Catherine looked pale and gaunt. Her hair was pulled back, and there was an angry-looking rash behind one of her ears. She looked at Marina without expression. "So you came," she said.

Marina put down her suitcase. "I came to take you home."

"I am home."

"We have to talk, Catherine."

Catherine's lips curved. "Wait here," she said, and went into the house's shadowy interior.

Marina waited a long time, facing the road. Down the way, at a vegetable stand, a mound of oranges looked molten in the fierce light. The group of children at the gate slowly dispersed. A man in a white dhoti drove a herd of goats past, their bleats lost in the cloud of dust raised by their hooves. From somewhere came a drone she recognized: *Guru Nagarajan, Parama Sukhadam. Guru Nagarajan, Chrana Shranam.*

At last a skinny young man with short brown hair and pimples appeared in the doorway. "Come with me," he said.

She followed him through a room that was empty except for rolled mats against the wall, and down a short hallway. He stopped in front of a door across which a curtain hung, motioned to her to wait, and went inside. She heard low voices. In a moment he emerged and said, "You can go in."

The shuttered room was close, but not as hot as Marina had expected. On a low table was a statue of a Hindu god—Shiva, the destroyer, she later learned, the god who garlanded himself with cobras. Marigolds littered the table in front of the statue, and their faint fresh odor mingled with the heavier smell of incense. Nagarajan reclined on one elbow on a mat on the floor. He smiled when he saw her and sat up gracefully. "You have come to see me. Most delightful," he said. He waved his hand at another mat. "Please."

As Marina sat down she said, "I didn't come to see you. I came to take my sister home."

Nagarajan looked interested. "Yes," he said. "But have you never set out to buy apples, and when you reached the market found that the pears were more beautiful, so bought pears instead? Have you never set out for the ocean, but found the mountains so interesting you stayed in the mountains? Of course you have."

"I'm not changing my mind."

"Perhaps not. I see you are very clear about what you want. The bitterest, most worm-infested apple, you say, is better than the plumpest, sweetest pear. I admire such single-mindedness."

"You make it sound like—"

"No, it is how you have heard it, not how I have made it sound."

Nagarajan's face was serious, but she saw a suspicion

of laughter in his eyes. His curly black hair, glossy and healthy-looking, fell to his shoulders. The mottled scar on his neck almost gleamed against his golden-brown skin. "I want to take my sister back home," she said.

He leaned toward her, and Marina smelled the not-unpleasant odor of his body. "We want and we want. That is where our trouble starts. Is it not so, Marina?" He reached out and, not actually touching her, outlined the side of her face with his fingers. She could feel the warmth emanating from his hand. "Isn't it?"

She felt heavy, unable to move. "Yes."

He withdrew his hand. "You will stay as our honored guest."

"I want to talk to Catherine."

"You will talk to Catherine. You see how easily wishes are granted? Yet granting one wish is like brushing one gnat from a piece of overripe fruit. What is one gnat out of a swarm?"

"When can I see her?"

He made a sweeping gesture. "Whenever you choose. Now. Tonight. Tomorrow. All of these. You have simply to ask her."

Marina got to her feet. "I'll do that."

He bowed over his pressed-together palms. "Welcome to Halapur."

"You are sad?" said Vijay.

Marina finished her beer. The combo was playing "The Isle of Capri." "I was thinking about when I first went to the ashram. I should have known Catherine would be beyond my reach. The problem wasn't my having a chance to talk to her, but her being willing to talk to me."

"She was lost to you already."

"Lost." She shook her head. "My God, Vijay. What if Nagarajan is alive?"

"You must not speak like this." Frowning, he fidgeted with the red foil matchbook from the ashtray.

"You're thinking it's time to call Mr. Curtis."

"Yes."

She considered, then said, "Can't you give it a little longer? We haven't tried to figure out who the others mentioned in the register are. Anand Kumar, the one who made the call. Vincent Shah, too. We won't push the Nagarajan angle. Let's see where the rest leads."

Vijay shook his head. "I don't know."

"Vijay, if it weren't for you we wouldn't have gotten this far. Don't call a halt now, before we know what's going on. Please."

His consent was grudging. "All right."

Good. The two of them would concentrate on Anand Kumar and Vincent Shah. She didn't have to tell him about any private plans she might make. Those she could keep strictly to herself.


Marina sat cross-legged on her bed in the Rama. Enough moonlight sifted into the room for her to be able to see the dial of her watch. It was three in the morning. Her packed suitcase sat next to the door with her canvas shoulder bag and her sandals on top of it. She'd decided to go barefooted, to cut down noise. An hour had passed since she had heard anyone stirring. The throat-clearing of the other guests had ceased, and the radio downstairs was silent. The bed groaned as she slid off it and crossed the room to the dressing table, where her flashlight, screwdriver, Swiss Army knife, and the plastic card for her automatic bank teller were laid out. She put the screwdriver and knife in separate pockets of her loose cotton pants so they wouldn't hit against each other. The flashlight and card she kept in her hand. She stood for a few moments gazing at her barely distinguishable reflection in the blistered mirror, then left the room, leaving the door unlocked and slightly ajar.

A feeble bulb cast a pool of yellow light in the stairwell at one end of the hall. At the other end was an open window that led, she had discovered a few hours ago, to a fire escape whose bottom few steps had rusted away. She moved silently toward the stairwell, feeling the rough material of the carpet runner under the soles of her feet. The smell of insecticide reminded her of bugs, and the thought made her toes curl.

Climbing the stairs earlier, after leaving Vijay, she had noticed that the fifth stair from the top creaked loudly. She avoided it on her way down. At the foot of the stairs she could turn left toward the door to the lobby, from which a faint night light was shining, or go right and make her way down a now-unlit passage that led to the office and, beyond that, to what she guessed were the quarters for the staff. She had looked into the passage earlier, when the lights were on, and had seen three empty Campa Cola bottles along one wall. She stayed clear of them. When she was well into the passage she pushed the button on her little flashlight and the beam showed her the closed door of the office.

She allowed herself an instant to hope nobody was sleeping on the other side before she maneuvered the door's flimsy lock open with her bank card. The door opened almost noiselessly, and she felt the day's trapped heat on her face. She stepped quickly into the room, shone the light around to make sure nobody was there, and closed the door behind her.

Her light flickered over wooden crates stacked along one wall, a desk piled with papers, a bicycle frame without wheels. Next to the desk was the battered tin trunk where the old woman had said Raki kept his papers. She knelt beside it. Locked, of course, but is that a problem for a lady engineer? She propped the light to shine on the lock and got out her screwdriver. No problem at all. This is something I can deal with, for a change.

Screws tight. Put a little body English on it. There. Now the other one. She removed the lock, placed it on the floor, and opened the trunk.

The pages from the register on top. Get those out of the way, and we've got—more paper. The trunk was jammed with file folders. She pulled one out. Bill receipts, with "Hotel Rama" imprinted at the top. Have I gone to all this trouble just to rifle the Rama's back files? Another folder, and another, held more of the same. Marina pushed moist hair off her forehead and sat back on her heels.

Try here at the back. This folder had more paper, more incomprehensible notations, but these were written on sheets headed "Elephanta Trading and Tours" and decorated with a sketch of the head of a smiling elephant. There's a poster for Elephanta in the lobby, too. I could make some inquiries about Elephanta Trading and Tours.

None of this was what she really wanted, but soon she found it. A folded piece of paper was half-wedged in a crack where two sides of the trunk met the bottom. She unfolded it and found herself staring into the eyes of

Nagarajan. It was a copy of the poster that had hung on the walls of the San Francisco ashram, the larger version of the picture Catherine had in her bedroom. Under the beam of her light first one eye and then the other flashed at her, then the full mouth was illuminated. She switched the light off and refolded the poster in the dark, not wanting to look at it any more.

What does this mean, really, Vijay will say. You knew he stayed here. He left a poster. So what. I'll say, so Raki kept it. Here, where he keeps important things. Raki told the toothed rope. Raki keeps a picture of Nagarajan.

She switched the light back on and, fumbling, suddenly in a hurry, screwed the lock back into place. Damn that picture. In her rush to get away, she bumped into the bicycle frame, which thudded against the wall. Oh no.

As she was going out the door she heard another door close, and Raki's scraping steps in the passage. She rushed toward the stairs. Forgetting the cola bottles lined up near the wall, she kicked one, knocking over the others. Raki's steps quickened, and she ran. At the top of the stairs she glanced over her shoulder and saw him at the bottom. He glared at her, his face distorted, and started to haul himself laboriously up by the bannister. She ran down the hall, accompanied by the sound of his thumping climb. From behind one of the doors came sleepy, inquiring voices. She reached in the door of her room, grabbed her suitcase, bag, and sandals, and ran for the window at the opposite end of the hall as Raki reached the top of the stairs and started toward her.

Pushing her suitcase through the window ahead of her, she climbed out. Raki shouted, a hoarse roar in a language she didn't understand. The rusting steps scraped the bottoms of her feet as she ran down.

Raki cried out again, and a light came on in the window next to the bottom of the fire escape, but the curtain didn't move as she dropped her suitcase to the ground and jumped down behind it. White-clad figures, huddled asleep in the alley, stirred as she passed. Finally, she was out on the street. Barefooted, her suitcase banging against her legs, she ran as fast as she could away from the Hotel Rama.

The mother and baby who had been sleeping near Marina on the floor of the Victoria Terminus stirred, and the baby began to fret. Other sleepers, too, made tentative, restless movements. Dawn was coming. Marina leaned her head back against the wall.

She had stumbled through the unfamiliar streets a long time before she dared stop even to put on her sandals. When she slowed to a walk, panting, convinced at last that nobody was following her, she happened across the extravagant, minareted railway station. It would be as good a shelter as any. She chose a place next to the wall, propped her suitcase beside her, wrapped her arms around her bag, and settled down to wait out the night. Sometimes she dozed for a few moments. More often she tried to think, her brain circling ceaselessly, monotonously.

Nagarajan escaped from the Halapur jail. He's alive. I should've realized he'd never kill himself. Not if there was anybody left he could con. No, he's out there, somewhere. On Elephanta, maybe. Catherine is with him, or he knows where she is.

Marina was supposed to meet Vijay at ten o'clock at the Rama. She'd have to alert him not to go there, and that meant telling him what she'd done. He wouldn't be pleased. I've screwed this up, just like I screwed up the Loopy Doop investigation. She looked at her scratched and filthy feet, the smudges of dirt on her pants. Pathetic.

A train came in, causing a flurry of activity among the lounging porters, and in a few minutes the disembarking passengers streamed past. One of the men hurrying by, gray-haired, wiry, clutching a bulging briefcase, reminded Marina of Professor Chaudhuri.

That was back in the days when she still thought Catherine could be swayed by rational argument. She had seen the professor in his office in the Institute for Asian Research at Berkeley. Hoping for ammunition, she had asked him if he had ever heard of Nagarajan.

"Most certainly I have heard of nagas," the professor said, in a precise British accent. "They are an ancient and powerful part of Indian religion and culture. As for this fellow calling himself Nagarajan—a common name in South India—I have not heard of him. That means very little. I don't investigate every so-called holy man who comes searching for followers and money in the gullible West."

"You sound as if you don't approve."

He shrugged. "Some are sincere, some are outright charlatans. From what you tell me of this Nagarajan, he has picked a few elements out of Indian tradition, mixed them with a great amount of mumbo jumbo, and is using it to snare unwary searchers such as your sister."

"So there's no basis—"

"Indeed there is a basis," he said, sounding annoyed. "That is what exists. A basis. Serpent-worship was one of our earliest religions, and it continues today."

His eyes unfocused slightly, and Marina thought he was moving into a lecture he had given before. "Nagas are associated with water—pools, wells, and so on. Supposedly, they live beneath the earth in a kingdom called the Nagaloka, where they guard a huge treasure of gold and precious gems. They take human form when they choose, but they are most definitely animal, and belong to the serpent world.

"Consider the serpent," said Professor Chaudhuri, now intent on his subject. "Where else but in the serpent do you find such a combination of the dangerous and the auspicious? The serpent is deadly; his bite kills. Yet, he sheds his skin, a symbol of rebirth. He raises himself, like the phallus, and so is a symbol of fertility. He is feared, yet considered a good omen. The naga, then, is the cobra who has become a divine being."

"And there are people who really believe—"

Professor Chaudhuri held up his finger to silence her. "In art, you will recognize the naga by the hood or umbrella of serpents which frames his head like a halo. The upper body is human, the lower is snake. In Hindu religion, the cobra is associated with Shiva, the destroyer, and Shiva is often depicted as garlanded with snakes. Shiva's symbol, the lingam, is a stone of phallic shape, another serpent association. We have also Sesha, the World Serpent, who holds the earth in his coils. There is a great deal more besides."

He looked as if he would be glad to continue, but Marina didn't encourage him. She had gained one paramount impression from his remarks. "It sounds as if Nagarajan has tapped into something with real power behind it." She felt let down, as if Professor Chaudhuri had destroyed one of her most cherished illusions.

"Indeed he has," the professor said.

\* \* \*

Light from outside was getting stronger, and the station was beginning to bustle with early-morning activity. Marina rubbed her face. Her eyes felt gummy, her body weary and sore. She dragged her suitcase to the rest room and rinsed her face and hands, then drank a cup of tea at the tea stall while she considered her next move.

She felt a great longing for comfort, for insulation, for something that was the opposite of the Rama. Once, on a day she wouldn't think about right now, she had taken a bus tour of Bombay. Herded out of the bus with her fellow tourists at the Gateway of India, she had looked across the road to a palace, all curved lines and arcades, that seemed, in her state of wound-up anxiety, to represent an unattainable, dreamlike tranquility. She left the station and got a minicab to the Taj Mahal Hotel.

Several hours later, she had showered and washed her hair in copious hot water, taken a nap, and eaten breakfast. As she dressed, she looked out the window of her room in the Taj toward the imposing stone arch of the Gateway of India overlooking Bombay harbor. The area around the Gateway was swarming with hawkers, food-sellers, and tourists. Crowds waited at the water's edge to get on tour boats for excursions to Elephanta. Watching the brightly painted, roofed, open-sided boats come and go, she thought about Raki's Elephanta Trading and Tours papers with their jolly elephant logo. She wouldn't know what to look for if she went there, but maybe— The phone rang, and it was Vijay calling from the lobby. Now she'd have to explain why she'd moved, as she promised she would when she'd called him earlier.

She found him sitting looking at a scribbled-over piece of paper, tapping the end of his pen against his teeth. He was as sartorially perfect as yesterday, this time in beige linen, and seemed excited and pleased with himself. "I have discovered something," he said. "I have been all morning with the map of Ahmedabad, where Anand Kumar wrote in the register that he lived, and with the telephone. I have discovered conclusively that the address this Anand Kumar put down is false. Such a street does not exist in Ahmedabad. What I am thinking is, perhaps the name is false also."

Marina sat beside him. "You mean it's a dead end? We won't be able to trace the call?"

"Not at all, not at all. You remember that underneath Anand Kumar's name, in Raki's hand, was written the name Vincent Shah, of Delightful Novelty Company. Now, I believe that this man registered as Anand Kumar, but that Raki discovered that his real name was Vincent Shah, and he wrote it underneath. Do you see?"

"How would Raki find out he'd given a false name?"

"The man wanted to call the States. Raki was worried about payment. Perhaps he searched the man's room, or somehow found a piece of identification. From what we've seen of him, I'm sure he would be capable of learning such a thing."

Of course he would. "What you're saying is Anand Kumar is Vincent Shah, so we look for Vincent Shah."

"Yes. I have found already that Delightful Novelty Company exists, and that a man named Vincent Shah works there."

"Fantastic." He looked so triumphant, his dark eyes shining behind his glasses, that she had to smile. The expression felt odd, unaccustomed. It was pleasant, this

114

moment when she and Vijay beamed at each other. It was a shame to spoil it.

"I got into some trouble last night."

His face clouded. "What happened?"

He looked increasingly pained as she described breaking into Raki's office and going through his files. As she described her flight from the hotel, he removed his glasses and rubbed his eyes. "This is very bad, Marina. I won't say you shouldn't have done it, since you know that. It puts me in an awkward position."

"Surely you don't think Raki's going to complain to the consulate?"

"No, but you have gotten into a dangerous situation, which is exactly what I was assigned to prevent. I think I must ask Mr. Curtis to have someone else take over."

She'd expected remonstrations, warnings, but not desertion. What was this wrenching sensation, the pleading tone that entered her voice so unexpectedly? "You can't. We're getting somewhere. In Raki's chest there's a picture of Nagarajan. There's a connection. You can't deny that, can you?"

He put his glasses back on and studied the knee of his slacks, with its crisp crease. "I don't want to encourage you on this course."

"It isn't a question of encouraging. What you say isn't going to change what I know is the truth. If you back out now, and get Mr. Curtis upset, you'll make things harder for me than they were before you started to help."

Vijay said nothing and didn't look at her. *He's going to dump me.* All the frustrations of the past weeks seemed to have rolled themselves into a ball and lodged in the back of her throat. *To hell with him. I never wanted him* around in the first place, with his pretty-boy clothes and his enthusiasm.

"You weren't honest with me," he said.

She shook her head, staring at her clenched fists in her lap.

"I can't help you if you do things behind my back, can I?"

"No." She flung the word out.

Another silence. Then he said, "Suppose we do this. You will tell me your plans, which will not include breaking into places, and I won't report to Mr. Curtis just yet. We'll continue just a while."

She wasn't sure she'd understood. When she looked at him he met her eyes with a small, inquiring smile.

It's silly to feel this relieved. "All right."

"Now, what shall we do?" he asked.

"Let's call the Delightful Novelty Company and get an appointment to see Vincent Shah. Then, let's take a trip to Elephanta."

Monkeys skittered along the wall beside the steps and chased each other through the trees. One crouched and regarded Marina with bright black eyes and she stopped to look at him. Two women on their way downhill, brass water jars balanced on their heads, picked their way through the crowd climbing toward the cave temple.

According to a very correct secretary at the Delightful Novelty Company, Vincent Shah was away on a business trip and would be back in a week's time. Marina had said she'd call again, and she and Vijay crossed the road and plunged into the crowd surrounding the Gateway of India.

As soon as they approached the water's edge they were assailed by boys waving tickets and calling, "Elephanta? Elephanta?" The touts swirled around Marina. "Best price, madam. Best boat." The glittering expanse of the harbor was full of vessels—not only the gaudy Elephanta tour boats, but huge tankers with rust-streaked sides, sailboats, fishing smacks. As Vijay negotiated for the tickets, Marina had the inexplicable feeling that she was on vacation, and she and Vijay were friends out for a pleasant afternoon's excursion. That she believed Nagarajan was alive and was going to Elephanta to search for his traces seemed like a bothersome detail she could almost ignore in the bright sun, with the air full of whirring mechanical pigeons and salt water.

When they found a seat on the open-sided, flat-bottomed boat Vijay took off his jacket and slung it over his shoulder, and Marina could see the holiday atmosphere had affected him too. Like a tour guide, as the boat slid away he pointed to an equestrian statue near the Gateway and said, "That is Shivaji, a great warrior and hero of the Hindus."

She had heard the name. The memory of tumbled rock seen through the greasy window of a bus came back to her. "Didn't he and his followers have forts in the hills not far from Halapur?"

"Quite right. It is too bad, really. Once that land was Shivaji's kingdom. Now it is the home of thieves and bandits, these gangs of dacoits."

"What do they steal?"

"Whatever they can. They terrorize villages, sometimes they kidnap also. I myself call them simple thieves, but some claim political basis—against caste, or the tyranny of the rich. One named Baladeva is said to be

117

the Robin Hood of India—at least by some of the newspapers."

"Does he rob from the rich and give to the poor?"

"Certainly he robs from the rich. I think that is the only similarity. Although the poor people, because they are ignorant and probably afraid, do venerate him. Sometimes he comes from his stronghold in the hills and shows himself openly in the villages. The people bring him food and gifts."

"Why doesn't he get arrested?"

"That is the question they are asking in Parliament also."

They had chatted companionably throughout the trip. Vijay talked about his life, which included, in addition to his job, seeing a great many films and going to parties with what he called his "set."

Vijay was calling from up ahead, but Marina continued to stare at the monkey, unwilling to continue. All her good spirits were gone. *Don't be stupid. There's nothing else to do, only a snack bar down below, no sign of Elephanta Trading and Tours. Why not climb up to see the cave temple the island's famous for?* Vijay had suggested it. "We must see the temple. It is a Shiva temple, very ancient, very beautiful. Who made it and when, nobody knows for sure."

"A Shiva temple?" Disquieted, she had almost refused, suggested they get the next boat back, but Vijay looked so eager she consented.

As they ascended, her breathing began to speed up more than was warranted by the mild exertion. "We're almost there. Not much farther," Vijay called now, laughing at her slow progress. She waved at him and resumed her leaden climb.

The steps widened, stone elephants marking their borders, and ended in a broad courtyard. The temple was carved out of the rock of the hill, its low columns stretching back into the cave. Small groups straggled through it after guides, and people wandered individually or in twos and threes.

Marina conquered an impulse to turn and run. It was ten years ago. I'm back in India, and there are lots of Shiva temples in India. I was bound to see one sometime.

She followed Vijay past the stone doorkeepers into the twilight of the cave. He led her from one to another of its large sculpted panels depicting Shiva in various guises: as half man, half woman; killing a demon; as Nataraja, king of dancers; as the bringer of the Ganges to earth. Vijay told her their significance, obviously repeating stories he had known from childhood.

They stopped in front of a huge three-part face which loomed out of the rock. "This is the most famous," said Vijay. "People say Brahma is creator, Vishnu preserver, Shiva destroyer. Here, Shiva has all three aspects."

"The serpent is most beloved of Shiva," whispered Nagarajan. Marina blotted her face.

Dazed, she walked with Vijay to the temple's central enclosure, which contained a cylindrical stone shaft, rounded at the top. "That is the lingam, symbol of Shiva," Vijay said. "It represents the phallus, but also the sacred fire."

\* \* \*

Nagarajan was kneeling beside her bed mat in the darkness. He was naked, his penis erect. "You will come with me, Marina," he said.

Surely she hadn't gone with him. But yes, she had gone. His room smelled of incense. She remembered his hair falling around her face, and a feeling like showers of sparks igniting, burning, fading beneath her skin. His voice spun a melodic web inside her head. "The serpent is beloved of Shiva," he whispered. "It can stand by itself"—he laughed and indicated his penis—"which means it is very powerful." He had tasted like unknown spices, and his body was strong and sinuous. The dweller in the deep well, the guardian of the great treasure. Nagarajan, Eternal Giver of Happiness.

She was falling. She put her hands to her face.

She and Vijay stood on an outcropping of rock bordered by a low stone wall. Across the water was distant Bombay. "I should have thought," said Vijay. "Of course we should not have come here."

"I betrayed my sister. Betrayed her in every way." Marina's face felt hot and swollen. "I played both sides. I told her Nagarajan was a fraud, I complained to the consulate. I swore every day that I would leave, would never go to him again. But at night—"

"No, please. You must not tell me this."

"At night, I couldn't stop myself from going, and she knew it, all of them knew it. He'd had them all, played with them. Do you know what? If he had had a little more time, if he hadn't been arrested, I would have been dressing in saris and chanting along with the rest of them. I probably would've stood by while he killed Agit More. I probably would've helped him."

"Please—"

"Somebody saw a pariah dog dragging Agit More's head down Palika Road. They found the rest of him buried beside the house. Buried so shallowly dogs could dig him up. Maybe Nagarajan was trying to prove he could raise the dead, but the dogs beat him to it."

"Marina, I—"

"I could've gotten Catherine out before it happened. I could've dragged her out, but I waited and waited because I couldn't quite bear to give him up just yet—"

"I will not listen to this, Marina!" Vijay lips were trembling. He turned his back and walked a few steps away from her.

Marina leaned against the wall, feeling the cool stone beneath her hands. Perspiration made a liquid track past one of her ears.

"I'm sorry," she said.

"You said horrible things." His voice was choked.

"I'm sorry."

He turned toward her again. "You are determined to find him."

"I'm determined to know what's going on."

"How can you find out?"

She hadn't thought about it, but the words came. "I'll go back to Halapur. Talk to the people there, the guard at the prison . . ." Her voice trailed off.

His shoulders sagged. "Perhaps it is time to leave. Shall we return to the boat?"

They didn't speak on the way down the hill. His face, when she glanced at it, looked solemn and closed. She had struggled never to think of what had happened between her and Nagarajan. When she discussed it with Clara, she was detached, clinical. Patrick didn't want to talk about it. She had never before been so possessed by the memory.

Attempting to ease the strain, she said, "Do you think the people at the snack bar have heard of Elephanta Trading and Tours?"

"Perhaps I should ask before we leave." Vijay's tone was courteous but distant. When they reached the landing stage she waited on the ramshackle dock while he talked with the elderly man who ran the ice cream stand.

He joined her in a few minutes and said, "That was easy enough. Elephanta Trading and Tours is the company responsible for bringing supplies over to the island. The agent in charge is a man with a twisted back and a club foot. His name is Raki."

The trip that had begun in unexpected enjoyment ended bleakly. They disembarked at the Gateway of India and walked silently back across the street to the hotel. In the lobby Vijay said, abruptly, "I must leave for an appointment. Tomorrow morning we go to Halapur. The driver and I will be here at seven-thirty."

"You're coming with me?"

"Why not, since it is my job to accompany you?" His tone was remote.

"You're obviously feeling—"

"How I feel does not enter in."

"Vijay—" She was at a loss. "Can you come have tea, or a drink?"

He checked his watch. "I must go to my other commitment."

It was no use. "I'll see you tomorrow, then."

She watched him walk briskly away. Give me a break, Vijay. I know you're prim and proper and I shouldn't have babbled on about having sex with Nagarajan, but just—give me a break. Don't you think I would've shut up if I could?

She went to her room and collapsed on the bed, letting the air-conditioning dry the perspiration from her skin. Tomorrow, Halapur. It was the next obvious move. There was one Bombay lead she hadn't followed up, though. Joginder. He might know something, but even if he didn't she should find him, see how he was. He had saved her from the mob, from the sight of the burning ashram. She went downstairs and had the doorman call her a taxi.

Although she had visited Joginder in Bombay before she left the last time, she didn't remember much about the place where he had lived with his brother except that it was in a warren of tin-roofed houses off the road to the airport. The driver grunted when she described it and pulled into the clogged traffic, where red double-decker buses, bicycles, motorbikes, ox-carts, and cars competed for space.

She stared out the window, unable to escape Nagarajan's image. Knowing his power he had toyed with her, playing on her desire and despair. His beauty, perfect except for the mottled scar at the base of his throat, was addictive, dangerous. Angry at her helplessness, she had focused on the scar. Because he didn't want her to touch it, she had always tried to, and never succeeded. Even overcome by passion, even asleep, he would push her fingers away. It was a game she'd played, and like every game she played with him, she'd lost. She tried to concentrate on anything else. A tree with fiery blossoms. A woman in a green sari, shading herself from the sun with a white umbrella.

The driver slowed and looked at her inquiringly, and she recognized the place. He turned into the winding dirt street and she knew the way without having to stop and ask. When they pulled up in front of the house, with its packed-earth yard and sagging frame of weathered, unpainted wood, she asked the driver to wait and crossed to the open door.

She rapped on the door frame, then peered inside. A woman with long, loose hair, holding a naked baby, pulled the baby closer and stared at her. In a corner an older woman crouched.

"I'm looking for Joginder. Joginder?" She wished for Vijay and his command of the language.

She thought the younger woman understood. She beckoned Marina in and led her to a back door opening on a tiny courtyard. In a corner, squatting in the dust, was a figure Marina barely recognized as Joginder.

His face looked caved in, and his mouth moved in a ceaseless mumble as his hands twisted and writhed. He did not look up as she approached. "Joginder?" she said, but he continued to mutter and stare in front of him.

She crouched down. "It's Marina. From the ashram, remember?"

"He rarely speaks."

She looked up, startled, into the face of a man who bore a strong resemblance to Joginder. She had, she remembered, met Joginder's brother briefly when she came here before. "I'm—"

"I remember you." The man's face was bony and handsome, but his eyes looked tired. "You were here long ago."

She got to her feet. "Yes. Then, I came to thank Joginder for helping me. I was hoping to talk with him again."

A small distortion of his mouth was gone an instant later. "He is as you see him. After he came from Halapur, he changed. For years now he cannot work. He must be led like an animal from place to place. His wife, his children, have gone to another. What could she do? We could help only a little."

"Does he ever speak?"

"From time to time. But he speaks only to his guru."

"His guru?"

"Sri Nagarajan."

Marina fought to keep her voice steady. "Are you saying—"

"I am saying that he speaks as if to someone, but there is only air. He speaks as if Sri Nagarajan were before him."

"What does he say?"

"He says, over and over, that he will be faithful, he will keep the great secret. That is all."

"Keep the secret?" She plunged ahead. "Do you think he believes Nagarajan is still alive?"

"Who can say what he believes?"

Marina looked at the gibbering, dust-covered figure of the man who had led her away from the mob and the burning ashram. "He's been like this since he came from Halapur?"

"He changed slowly, but since that time he was never at ease in his mind."

Never at ease in his mind. Both of us running away from the fire. "I'd like to give you something toward his care."

"You are kind, but he is my brother. It is for me to look after him."

She tried to insist, but Joginder's brother impassively refused as they walked to the door. When they said goodbye, he said, "I am sorry you do not find him better. I still hope—he is my brother. But I begin to think he will not be better in this life."

She woke the taxi driver, who was dozing behind the wheel, and told him to take her back to the Taj. Nagarajan had claimed another victim.

Marina ate a hasty breakfast of toast and coffee from room service, took the newspaper from her tray, and went downstairs to wait outside for Vijay. The early-morning air was cool, with only a hint of the sultriness that would come later. Joginder had been in her thoughts since the previous afternoon. *He speaks only to his guru. He says he will be faithful. He will not give away the great secret.*

She had never believed Joginder to be one of Nagarajan's devotees. Her impression was that he regarded his work as a job, not a religious vocation. Something must have convinced Joginder that Nagarajan did indeed have great power. Something like Nagarajan appearing to Joginder after Joginder had been told he was dead. He would have used Joginder's awe and fear to elicit whatever he wanted—help in getting out of Halapur, possibly.

A car pulled up. Vijay was sitting in the back seat with

his briefcase on his knees. His smile when he saw her was perfunctory. "So. It will take us two hours," he said. He opened his briefcase, got out his pen, and began looking at and making notations on papers.

I'm not going to cajole him. She settled in her corner of the back seat and read the newspaper accounts of a train derailment that had left twenty dead, the parliamentary outcry over the temerity of the dacoit Baladeva, the burning of the huts of untouchables. By the time she looked up, they had left the industrial environs of Bombay and were crossing a rocky plain. She remembered the scenery from the bus trips she had taken between Halapur and Bombay to visit the consulate. The car met a bus, and as it flashed by she searched the windows as if for a trace of her former self, but no pale, strained face looked back at her.

"There. You see? It is a fort. There, on top of the hill."

Vijay had decided to talk. When she followed his pointing finger she saw the rocky ruins. "One of Shivaji's?"

"I think so."

He was putting his papers away. "You're through with your work?"

"One is never through with work. For the moment, yes."

Try a little conversation. "How did your appointment go yesterday afternoon?"

His face closed. "It went well." He looked out the window for several minutes, then said, "My parents have found a wife for me. I met her yesterday." His tone held no enthusiasm.

"Congratulations. What's her name?"

"Sushila."

"She's pretty?"

"Very pretty. Just finishing at university. Specializing in biology."

"She sounds nice."

"Very nice." Vijay drummed his fingers on his knees. It was impossible to ignore his disquiet. "Don't you want to get married?"

Vijay frowned. "It is suitable that I marry. I want to please my parents. I want to have children. Yet sometimes I feel there is still much to do, to see. I feel that once I am married I will stay in my corner of Bombay only." He was, she saw, even more upset than she had imagined. "My father says I have been too much with the Americans. That these are American ideas."

"A lot of Americans do feel that way about—being tied down."

"Exactly! Tied down!" he burst out. "We shall live with my parents, as the custom is. I shall come home from work at night, and my wife will tell me of the terrible things my mother did to her. Then my mother will take me aside to tell me that my wife is slovenly, or lazy, or doesn't look after the children properly. Then my wife will tell me—" He put his hands over his ears, as if to shut out the imagined voices.

"You don't know it will be like that."

"It is always quarrelling, always rivalry."

"I don't believe you. If it were that awful, people wouldn't have been living that way for thousands of years." Who am I to be arguing in favor of matrimony? Patrick would laugh if he could hear me.

Vijay looked so woebegone she had to smile. He

shook his head, his own smile rueful. "I do not want to get married."

"That's obvious."

"Sushila is a pretty girl, a good girl, but if I were choosing, I might choose—someone very different."

"Do you have to go through with it?"

"The astrologer is studying his charts to pick the most auspicious day. Everyone except me is very happy."

"That doesn't answer my question."

"I do not know the answer to your question."

They fell into a companionable silence. In half an hour or so Marina recognized the outskirts of Halapur.

Ten years had made no difference. Women still sat outside their roadside lean-tos and wove baskets of long, supple, white-yellow rushes. It could have been the same broken shutter that hung loosely from one of the windows of the District Administration Center, the same bullocks that nosed in the brown stubble of its garden. In the central square the peepul tree spread its branches, and in its shade small groups of men crouched, chewing betel and talking about—what? Marina had always wondered. At the public pump women with their water jars laughed and talked, their saris bright, bangles gleaming on their arms.

The bus had stopped here. It was down one of the little streets leading off the square—Marina picked out the one immediately—that she had walked to reach Palika Road and the ashram. She could remember every turn of it. The barber shop, where customers reclined while the barber scraped their faces with his straight razor; the temple, with the maimed or blind beggars in its precincts; the shop with saris hanging outside, rustling in whatever breeze reached its cramped confines—

"Marina? I was asking where you would like to go."

The car had stopped, and Vijay and the driver were looking at her. The starting point had to be the last place Nagarajan had been seen alive, the place where he was supposed to have died. "Let's go to the police station," she said.

When Marina had last been in the Halapur police station, she had said she didn't want Catherine's ring with the pink stone, and the man had put the piece of misshaped metal into a brown envelope. He had watched her guardedly, as if afraid she would suddenly scream, cry, accuse, not knowing how little chance of that there was. She could no more have wept or raised her voice than she could have touched the ring. She had thanked him and walked out of the ugly orange stucco building with its flat roof and concrete arcades and extravagant masses of bougainvillea.

Her work had taken her to other police stations since then, and now she knew that the one in Halapur was completely typical. There was the long counter, the smell of paper and of strong cleanser, the bulletin board with its printed sheets, and the man behind the counter, who looked drowsy no matter what the time of day. He blinked as they came in, and sat up straighter.

"I think it will be better if I make our request," Vijay had said outside, and now he swept up to the drowsy man and spoke in Marathi, taking from his breast pocket an envelope from which he drew a sheet of official station-ery with a brief text, embossed stamps, and a signature endowed with loops and flourishes. The man glanced at it, then reached for the telephone near his elbow. While he spoke into it, Vijay picked up the paper and put it away.

The man hung up, said something to Vijay, and left the room. As they waited, Marina said, "What was that you showed him?"

"An official request for assistance with our inquiries into the incidents on Palika Road."

"But we don't have an official request."

"Now we do."

"Mr. Curtis signed the paper?"

"Well—" Vijay hesitated.

"Vijay—"

"I signed it myself. With my own name, of course."

Marina was aghast. Nothing could be more completely out of character. "You can't have! You'll get into trouble!"

"Suppose we came here and asked politely to inquire into the case. We would at this moment be walking out the door. Whoever reads the document carefully, which you have noticed he did not do, will see that it says, in very elaborate language, that we are doing this under the auspices of the consulate. It is not my fault if they do not read carefully. And besides," he went on fiercely, "suppose I do get into trouble. I have at least done for once what it was my own wish and decision to do."

Before Marina could answer the man returned and indicated that they should follow him. A short way down a hall he showed them into an office where a heavy man in shirtsleeves, with slick gray hair and a hanging underlip, was dictating to a secretary in a blue sari. He ignored them for several minutes before dismissing her with a gesture and turning to them.

"I am the chief of police. You wish to see me?"

"Vijay Pandit, of the American consulate in Bombay. Miss Robinson, here, is the sister of a girl killed on Palika Road in the ashram fire some years ago. We are looking into the circumstances surrounding that event." Vijay's manner had an overtone of pompousness.

The chief leaned back and plucked at his underlip. He didn't ask them to sit down. He looked at Marina. "What are you hoping to find, Miss Robinson?"

Marina tried to match Vijay's officious manner. "I've had indications recently that my sister is alive, that she somehow escaped the fire. I want to find out the exact circumstances."

"I see." He sat forward. "I cannot open our files to you unless you go to a great deal of legal trouble. I was, however, a junior officer here at that time, and I remember the incident well. I can tell you without doubt that no one could have escaped or survived. Fuel oil had been thrown into the blaze, and it was very hot. We found the remains of three bodies together in what we later learned had been the room set aside for meditation. In such cases identification is not easy, but we established to our own satisfaction and, as I recall, that of the consulate"—he glanced at Vijay—"the identities of the victims. I am sorry I cannot hold out any hope to you."

"And the—the guru, Nagarajan," Marina said. "He killed himself here, in jail. Are you familiar with the circumstances of his death, too?"

She wondered if she saw a slight ripple in his heavy jowls. His eyes didn't move. "No, I am not," he said. "I understand that he hanged himself in remorse. The guard found him when he came by on his rounds the night the ashram burned."

"The guard," Vijay said. "Is that guard here? Can we talk with him?"

"He no longer works here."

Vijay drew himself up. "We would like to have his name and whereabouts, if you know them." His tone implied that he was giving an order.

The chief's underlip pushed out farther, but he didn't protest. "He is called Baburao. He lives outside of town, on the Mahabaleshwar Road. Anyone will show you." He pulled some papers forward and bent over them. He did not raise his head as they left.

Back in the car, as the driver slowly made his way toward southern Halapur and the Mahabaleshwar Road, Marina said, "Did it strike you as odd that he remembered the guard's name immediately, and knew where he lived? Surely he would've forgotten, after all this time, and have had to look it up?"

Vijay shrugged. "Possibly. It is equally possible that it was such an important episode in his life that he never forgot."

Houses and shops began to thin out, and they stopped at a galvanized metal stand advertising Campa Cola and Kwality Ice Cream while the driver asked directions. "Another thing," Marina said. "Why is anybody in town going to be able to tell us how to find the house of some ex-prison guard? Do you think the police chief was just trying to get rid of us, hoping we'd spend the whole day searching?"

"That we shall see."

In fact, the driver seemed to tell Vijay he had gotten specific directions to Baburao's house. They crossed the river, low and sluggish in its banks. Women with their saris tucked around them stood in it calf-deep, pounding their washing on flat stones. Laundry was spread to dry on bordering bushes. Beyond them, a man washed his bullock, splashing water over the animal's neck and flanks.

Half a mile past the river they turned into a rougher road. They wound along, bouncing from side to side, toward a line of trees. When they reached the trees, Marina saw among them the house of Baburao.

It was two stories high, built of stone of a mellow golden color. Wooden balconies ringed the top floor, matching the wide wooden veranda on the bottom. Crows strutted through the stone-bordered garden. To one side of the house a bright red tractor was up on blocks. A dusty black car stood at the front steps.

Vijay's laugh was short and sardonic. "Now we see why everyone knows where Baburao lives. He must be one of the richest men in Halapur. The house looks new, too. He built himself the perfect British officer's cottage."

When they got out of the car, Marina heard the thin, far-off sound of wailing. The front door of the house, she noticed, was standing open. "Something's wrong," she said. The two of them hurried toward the house, crossed the veranda and entered a wide hall. A young woman rushed from a side door. When she saw them she shrieked and started to run the other way, but Vijay spoke to her rapidly and she stopped. Her face, Marina saw, was streaming with tears. She answered him with a few strangled syllables, then disappeared into the back of the house.

Vijay looked shaken. "Baburao is dead," he said. "His body was just found. The men have gone to bring it from the fields."

A low babble of voices came from outside, and Marina and Vijay went back out to the front yard. Straggling around the side of the house was a group of six or seven men, several of them supporting a limp figure on their shoulders. Marina could see long red scratches on one of the exposed calves of the dhoti-clad body. The head lolled, and she saw that one side of it was covered with blood, which had trickled across the face. One of the men was trying, without much effect, to brush away the cloud of flies that hovered around the wound. Beside the group and a little apart from it walked a man with a fringe of gray hair and steel-rimmed glasses. He wore dark trousers and an open shirt and carried a black bag.

As the men rounded the side of the house the wailing, which had gone on continuously, grew louder, and a woman with her gray hair undone burst from the front door, shrieking and crying. Several other women followed, including the one Vijay had stopped in the hall. When the gray-haired woman saw the body she gave a long, loud cry and fell to her knees, sobbing. The women and the doctor gathered around her while the men, after a brief hesitation, carried the body up the steps and into the house. The doctor and the women succeeded in raising the gray-haired woman to her feet and half-dragged her after them. The sound of her cries was once again muffled in the interior of the house.

Nobody had taken notice of Marina and Vijay, standing to one side on the graveled path. When they were alone Marina asked, "Did she tell you what happened to him?"

"Only what I have said, that he is dead. We must find out more, I think?"

"We can't just go in and—"

"No, no, we must wait a little."

Vijay went to talk with the driver, who had parked the car under the trees a little distance away. Marina stood uncertainly in the garden. She had seen many grief-stricken people, but the woman's unrestrained outpouring left her abashed, almost ashamed of her next thought, which was that now Baburao wouldn't be able to help them. She studied the house. In terms of the way most people in India lived, it was a mansion. Ten years ago, Baburao had been a prison guard. He had risen rapidly.

Vijay returned, and he and Marina walked aimlessly through the garden. At last, someone emerged from the house. The doctor crossed the veranda and descended the steps to the black car. He noticed them and stopped, sunlight glinting on his glasses.

Vijay approached him and spoke in Marathi. The doctor answered, and when Vijay spoke again he responded, "Yes, I speak English. I studied medicine at Johns Hopkins in the United States." He took out a handkerchief and patted his high forehead. "You are friends of Baburao?"

"We didn't know him, but we wanted to talk with him," Marina said.

"A terrible accident. I can do nothing for him now."

"What happened?" asked Vijay.

"At some time during the night, Baburao left his house and walked out across his fields. In the dark, he must have stumbled and fallen into a steep gully that borders one of them. He hit his head against the rocks at the bottom. The farmer who works the field discovered the body this morning."

"Why would he go to the fields in the middle of the night?" Marina asked.

"No one can say. It was not for his bodily needs. He was most proud that he had put modern plumbing conveniences in his new house. Walking about at night was not his custom, his wife says. She retired before he did, and no one missed him until this morning. Even then, they thought he must be nearby. As he was."

The doctor got in his car. Vijay bent to the window and said, "We know that Baburao was formerly a guard at the prison. How did he become so wealthy?"

"Some years ago, he got money. He said it was from his relatives working in Iran, in the oil fields. With the money he bought land. He was a shrewd man. A thrifty man." The doctor started his car, made a gesture of farewell, and drove off, leaving Vijay and Marina in a cloud of swirling dust.

Marina heard a movement behind her on the veranda, and turned to see the young woman Vijay had questioned earlier. Her eyes were red, but she looked more composed, and Marina saw that she was beautiful, with huge dark eyes, full lips, and a waist-length braid hanging down her back. She spoke to Vijay in a low, strained voice. They exchanged several remarks before Vijay said to Marina, "I have told her we came to see Baburao on business. She is his daughter-in-law. She is apologizing that she cannot ask us to come in and take food."

Marina was amazed. "Apologizing, when they just found the man's body? Everything must be—"

"Yes, she apologizes, because it is our rule that guests, even unexpected ones, must be treated as if they are gods. She cannot offer us food because the dead body of Baburao has brought pollution into the house."

"Pollution?"

"Death is just one of many things that are considered to be polluting. The people in this house must undergo ritual cleansing before they can eat again."

The woman was looking curiously at Marina. She spoke to Vijay, and Vijay said, "She would like to know where you are from."

"Tell her I'm from California. San Francisco."

Vijay had several exchanges with the woman and then said, "She wants to know if California is a big place."

"Tell her it's very big."

Vijay spoke, and the woman replied. Toward the end of her speech her voice broke and she dabbed at her eyes with the end of her sari.

"She says that Baburao had promised to take the family to the States for a visit when her son was a little older," Vijay said.

Crying openly, the woman gasped out a few words at a time to Vijay. He nodded and murmured comments. At last, breaking down completely, she took refuge in the doorway.

"She was telling me about the last time she saw her father-in-law," Vijay said. "About midday yesterday a boy rode out from town on his bicycle with a message for Baburao. Baburao read the message and closed himself in his office all the afternoon. After dinner, he shut himself in his office again. Last night, before going to bed, she took him a cup of tea. He looked worn out. He said to her, 'Gita, you have been a fine wife to my son and have given me a good, strong grandson.' She was moved, and knelt to touch his feet and receive his blessing. It was the last time she saw him alive."

Gita, no longer crying, had moved toward them once

more, listening to Vijay's recitation with an interested expression. "Does she know what happened to the message? Or what it said?" Marina asked.

Vijay's expression didn't change as Gita answered his question, but Marina saw his body stiffen. When the woman finished speaking, his tone was casual. "Please do not show surprise or alarm when I tell you this. She says the message was open on Baburao's desk last night. She cannot read, but she says that on the top of the paper there was a picture of a smiling elephant. The paper is no longer in his office, and it was not found on his body."

To keep herself from reacting, Marina dug her nails into the palms of her hands. Elephanta Trading and Tours, Raki, Nagarajan. When she looked back at Vijay, she thought his face seemed pinched. "Does she know the boy who brought the message?" she asked.

After questioning Gita further Vijay said that she did not know the boy's name, but that he occasionally delivered messages to Baburao. He could often be found waiting for assignments near the peepul tree in the square in the center of Halapur.

They went through polite formulas of thanks and condolence. As they walked to the car Marina said, "It's Nagarajan again. You can't deny it."

"I don't deny it."

"He killed Baburao, or had him killed."

"It is likely."

"We have to find the boy with the bicycle."

As the car bounced away from the house Marina thought about Baburao. A thrifty man, a shrewd man, the doctor had said. He got money—from relatives in the

139

Iranian oil fields, or from Nagarajan as a bribe for his release? And because Baburao was shrewd and thrifty, he got rich. He built a house, inside which his dead body lay. Baburao was less than nothing now. Less even than a guard at the Halapur jail.

They turned toward Halapur, passing two men on the shoulder of the road who were smoking cigarettes and desultorily tinkering with a black motorcycle. They must have gotten it fixed, Marina thought a few minutes later when she heard a high-pitched whine and looked back to see them riding it, one crouched behind the other. They wore goggles, and the wind whipped their hair. Marina thought of the boy who must ride his bicycle all this way in the heat, five miles or more, to deliver messages to Baburao. At least between jobs he was able to sit under the peepul tree.

When they reached the square, however, there was no boy with a bicycle resting there, and Vijay's inquiries of the men chewing betel brought only vague answers about where he was and when he might return.

Marina tried to suppress her disappointment. "There's one more thing I need to do here. Maybe when I've done it he'll be back."

"What do you wish to do?"

It had been growing in her mind since their arrival in Halapur. "I want to see Agit More's family."

Vijay's face darkened. "Why must you do that?"

"I just want—you know, I just want to see if they need anything."

They wandered out of the shade of the spreading tree and looked at the women talking animatedly at the pump. "It is not good," Vijay said. "Agit More is nothing to do with you."

Across the square, shrieking children played a game with sticks. A donkey lumbered by carrying a load of clay water jars covered with netting. Two men lounged near a motorcycle. "It is something to do with me," she said.

"What is that?"

"The investigators thought Agit More's murder was a ritual killing. It didn't seem to have been done out of—of anger or anything. It was like a sacrifice—" Marina swallowed and persisted. "Nagarajan had to bind people to him closely, make them loyal. It was important to him. I think killing Agit More was a way of getting his disciples—"

"You think your sister knew about, or participated in, this sacrifice of Agit More. Is that it?" Vijay's voice was soft.

Marina nodded. One suffocating afternoon a dog had trotted down Palika Road with the dirt-encrusted head of Agit More in its mouth: *The serpent is dangerous. Its bite can kill.*

"How could I know what they'd do?" Marina burst out. "I was gone so much. They never told me anything. I couldn't have stopped them, could I?" She grasped Vijay's arm. "Could I?"

Chills racked her body, and she was only peripherally aware of Vijay's hand pulling her along, leading her into a narrow alley where he put his arms around her. "No, no you could not," he whispered.

She clung to him. When she could talk, she said, "I hate Catherine. I hate her."

"So, so, so." She felt his lips brush her forehead, his hands pass lightly over her hair.

Marina always told herself she had never seen Agit

More, knowing that she had seen him many times. He was surely one of the group of children who laughed and played in the street, their bony bodies looking as if they would snap at the lightest blow. He was one of the group who stared at her when she came and went, met her in the street, and followed her to the gate. Occasionally one of the braver ones dared to call "Hello!" If she responded, there was a chorus, "Hello!" "Hello!" "Hello!" "Hello!" as all of them said it.

She had certainly said hello to Agit sometime.

When the worst of the shaking passed she pulled back. Vijay released her. "We must not shock the people of Halapur. To embrace in public is not done in India. Would you like tea?"

Hunched over a steaming cup in a nearly empty tea shop, Marina said, "Suppose Nagarajan murdered Baburao. Why would he do it now?"

"Perhaps he wanted to keep Baburao from talking with us."

She considered. "That would mean he knows where we are, what we're doing."

"If your own theory is correct, and Raki is in communication with him, then of course he knows about us. Raki caught you breaking into his office. He knows your name. He has seen me with you. If Nagarajan hasn't guessed by now that we are searching for him, he is not very intelligent."

Nagarajan unaware of them was one thing. Nagarajan poised to strike was another. "Should we go to the police, tell them our suspicions about what happened to Baburao?"

"No." Vijay held up two fingers and ticked off his points. "First, we have only our suspicions, and the police chief is not well-disposed toward us. Second, how do we know that the police are not involved? Baburao could hardly have gotten Nagarajan out of prison and cremated another body by himself. If it becomes known that Nagarajan is alive, it will be a grave embarrassment for the Halapur police. We will say nothing to them.

"But"—he put his hand flat on the table—"I will tell you what we will do. We will speak to the family of Agit More, if you insist. We will talk with the boy on the bicycle. Then we must return to Bombay, for me to put this matter into the hands of Mr. Curtis. If this disappoints you, forgive me, but I cannot allow you to be endangered. I simply cannot."

He was right, Marina decided with a mixture of letdown and relief. They would tell Mr. Curtis everything. He might be willing, given the information they had uncovered, to start some sort of investigation. Vijay wouldn't continue, and she wouldn't go on without him. "Fine. We'll tell him."

Vijay looked happier. He pushed his chair back. "Shall we make a move?"

There was no breeze, and the heat and exhaust fumes were almost overpowering. Marina's face was tingling from exposure to the sun, and her arms were red. They threaded through traffic and street hawkers. The barber shop was still there, the barber clipping the nose hairs of a reclining customer. A legless, toothless old man at the temple gate stretched his palm to them, and Vijay gave him a coin. The sari shop now housed greasy-looking boxes of machine parts and tools, and for an instant or so Marina thought about Loopy Doop.

By the next turn, the thought had vanished. Ahead on the corner two men were grinding out glasses of cane juice at a mobile sugarcane press. She walked past them and looked down the street. She had come back to Palika Road.

The past never dies, Marina thought. How could I imagine I could rid myself of this place? To Vijay, she said, "It's just like before."

The night Agit More was killed, she had been in Bombay. She had needed to get away from the ashram, from Nagarajan, to reestablish her equilibrium—or so she had rationalized it.

After her usual fruitless visit to the consulate she had dawdled. Telling herself she had seen nothing of Bombay but the airport and the consulate, she had taken a bus tour with a group of other Americans. Most of the people on the bus were Texans on a package tour, and they spent a great deal of time, she remembered, comparing everything they saw to similar things in Texas—the Hanging Gardens to the public parks of Houston; the Jain Temple, with its white-clad priests and statues of bug-eyed gods, to the churches of Dallas; the Parsee Towers of Silence, where bodies of the dead were left for birds to devour, to the crematoriums of Fort Worth.

By the time the tour ended she had, as she had half planned, missed the bus for Halapur. She stayed the night at a hostel, sharing a room with a Canadian girl who talked about nothing but hashish. The caretaker's baby was ill and had cried for hours.

As she and Vijay walked along the road, she wondered, as she had thousands of times before, if she had sensed that something terrible was going to happen and stayed away to avoid involvement. Catherine had looked more taut than usual, but Marina guiltily attributed that to jealousy of Marina's being Nagarajan's current favorite in bed. Whether or not Catherine really resented it Marina had never known. She said nothing, but she rarely spoke to Marina anyway.

Nagarajan would taunt her about Catherine. "Why can you not be like your sister? When she hears the truth, she knows it. Such lovely hair she has, yellow as mustard blossoms. I want always women around me with hair the color of yellow flowers."

She knew she was slipping, losing ground, but she continued to go to him. "You see, you do like me, Marina," he said one night as they lay, filmed with perspiration, on his bed mat.

She turned away, filled with self-loathing. "Yes, I like you."

"You see—" Nagarajan leaned over to speak in her ear. His hair tickled her shoulder. "You are so worried, so angry. You are like a bullock who fears the sound of the bell tied around his own neck, and so will not bend his head to eat."

"You mean I won't bend my head so you can slip on the yoke."

He laughed. "You are on guard always. Only think. When a bullock submits to the yoke he has a place, he is of use, isn't he? And a wise bullock knows that the sound of his bell is only a noise he creates himself, and will bend his head to take what is before him."

When she turned back to him that night, as she inevitably did turn back to him, he said, "You will see that the bell is making music only."

\* \* \*

Marina and Vijay had reached the front gate of the ashram. No. The front gate of the house that stood where the ashram used to be. Three children ran chattering through the doorway, stopping short to stare when they saw Marina and Vijay.

"That's where it was," Marina said. She stared at the house that looked exactly like the other house, at the earth that showed no trace of past fires. She waited, and felt nothing. There was no reason to stay. She turned and pointed diagonally across the street. "That's where Agit More lived."

The More house was no different from the others, except that a yellow motorbike leaned against the side wall. As they drew nearer, the whine of a radio drifted through the open windows. Marina tapped on the front door, and a barefoot girl of eleven or so, wearing a loose faded blue dress with puffed sleeves, her thin legs and tousled short hair streaked with dust, opened it and peered out at them.

Vijay questioned and the girl answered shyly. She stood back for them to enter. "Her name is Kamala More. Her mother is at the market, and Kamala is here caring for her nephews. She says we may wait for her mother to return," Vijay said.

A baby with a fuzz of dark hair sat on the floor. A naked boy about a year old was making a clatter by banging a string of wooden beads against the side of a new-looking console-model television set. The radio, on a shelf, also looked new. Marina did not remember, from the time of Agit More's murder, any indication that his family was anything but very poor, but television sets and motorbikes were not within the reach of poor Indian families. It looked as if in the intervening years the fortunes of the Mores, like those of Baburao, had improved.

The girl motioned to them to sit on a string cot and stood to one side watching. The toddler wavered across the room to them, gnawing his beads, and Vijay offered him a finger. The boy's small hand closed over it and he stood swaying, regarding Vijay solemnly. Vijay chuckled. "He has a strong grip. A good, strong boy."

He'll be very good with his children. Marina saw Vijay in a year or so, married to Sushila, with a baby of his own. The thought was vaguely disturbing. To distract herself, she said, "I'm not sure the Mores need any help from me. Have you noticed?"

"Yes, I have." The little boy let go of Vijay's finger, lost his balance, and sat down abruptly. He transferred his attention back to his beads. "I cannot understand how a family like this can afford a motorbike. Or a television set."

He turned to Kamala and talked with her. It seemed to Marina that the girl answered proudly. Then he said, "She tells me these things are gifts from Uncle. Uncle gave her older brother the motorbike, so he could go to work at the factory. Uncle gave them the television, and many other things. They are very grateful to him."

"So they have a rich relative after all. I always thought the family was poverty-stricken."

"Not necessarily a relative. 'Uncle' is a term of respect. The children would call any male friend of the family 'Uncle.'"

Kamala left the room. When she returned, she held reverently three bangles of twisted gold. She displayed them as she spoke to Vijay. When she left the room again, Vijay said, "Those bangles were a gift to her mother from Uncle."

"Is Uncle her mother's lover, I wonder?"

"I don't know."

When the girl returned, he spoke to her again, and nodded at her response. "I asked her if she knew Uncle's name," he said to Marina. "She does. It's Baburao."

Of course. The shrewd and thrifty Baburao was unexpectedly generous with the family of Agit More. That was because he had let Nagarajan, Agit More's killer, go free. Did the More family know the reason for their good fortune, or did Baburao invent an excuse for watching over them and providing for them? What would happen to them now? The baby started to fret, and Kamala picked it up. Marina wondered if Baburao's guilt had extended to including them in his will. "Let's go. I don't want to be the one to tell them he's dead."

When they were outside, Marina said, "Agit's murder benefited his family. How ironic."

"Ironic, yes. Still, it is good they had something, after all their suffering."

They did not stop again at the site of the ashram. Palika Road would be with her always, Marina knew, but now it was like a place she had seen in a dream, or a photograph in an album she rarely opened.

When they reached the town square, a rusting bicycle was listing on its kickstand under the peepul tree. Sitting with his back against the tree was a curly-haired boy of about fifteen wearing shorts and a loose shirt, threadbare tennis shoes without laces, and no socks. His face brightened when he saw Marina and Vijay approach, and he jumped to his feet.

"Good day, madam," he said to Marina. "You have message to send?"

Marina had barely articulated "N——" when he said, "I see. You want silks and saris. I take you, no problem. Indian art. Ivory carvings. Brasses. Very artistic, very beautiful."

"We want—"

Still talking, he released the kickstand and rolled his bicycle toward the edge of the square. "Stones, madam. Garnet. Tigereye. Good price, too. My cousin. Come."

Marina raised her eyebrows at Vijay. If they agreed to inspect his cousin's wares, the boy might be more willing to talk. In any case, it was impossible to break into his monologue.

"Paintings. On palm leaf. On cloth. Miniatures, very artistic. Lacquer boxes with flowers, birds. You will like. You are from?"

Stunned by the barrage of words, Marina could hardly gather her wits to answer. "The United States. California."

"California. Is beautiful. You like Halapur?"

"I—"

"You come to Halapur, shop at Laxmi Emporium. My cousin. I am Hari."

Once he was assured that they were following him, Hari's patter slowed somewhat. Marina wondered how much she would have to spend before she could ask Hari about the customer who had sent him to Baburao's yesterday. Hari leaned his bicycle against the front of a building which a sign proclaimed to be the Laxmi Emporium and ushered them inside.

The jumble of merchandise seemed to include most of what Hari had promised. Brass statues of Shiva as king of the dancers gleamed next to embroidered shoulder bags. Saris were strewn on a counter near stacked bolts of bright-colored silk. A glass case held jewelry and loose semiprecious stones. Several men sat in the back of the shop, drinking tea and having what appeared to be a serious discussion. Hari waved, and one of them waved back. "My cousin," said Hari. "I will show you."

As they approached the counter, Marina said, "Actually, we were looking for you because we wanted to ask you a question."

"Yes? I will answer of course. But first—" He waved his hand delicately to indicate the contents of the store.

She picked up trinkets. Maybe Don would be amused by this fierce-looking, stilettolike brass letter opener, with its engraved handle and red leather sheath with a design stamped on it in gold. She chose a figured silk scarf, blue and lavender flowers on a light green background, for Clara. As she made each selection, Hari congratulated her on the fine quality of the item she had chosen.

Marina was wondering if Hari would be willing to talk for just a letter opener and a scarf when she saw the tigereyes. The necklace, in the glass cabinet, was a graduated semicircle of stones as big as or bigger than marbles, rich brown shot through with swirls of gold. Amid the gaudy disorder of the other objects they seemed self-contained, serenely beautiful. She admonished herself to stop looking at them before Hari caught on, and turned her eyes away. I don't even like jewelry that much. Badly strung, too, she saw as Hari whisked them out of the case. When she felt their cool weight around her neck, she knew she would buy them.

Vijay haggled briefly with Hari over the price and

succeeded in reducing it by a third. Hari's cousin appeared, bowing, to take her money and made a parcel of her purchases, which she slipped into her shoulder bag. When the business was complete, Hari said, "Shall we take some refreshment?"

They ate oozing sweets at a cafe next door, and when Marina asked Hari about the message he had taken to Baburao the day before he dropped his head back and gazed at the ceiling. "Yes, yes, I remember," he said. "Yesterday morning. I did not know him. I have not seen him before. He paid me to take a message to Baburao." His tone indicated finality.

After a moment's silence, Vijay said, "What did he look like, this man?"

Hari shrugged. "A man. He spoke well." Apparently dissatisfaction with the description showed in their faces, because after a moment he continued, "He was small, also. His body was twisted."

Marina and Vijay exchanged glances. Raki himself had come to Halapur.

Hari smiled uncertainly. "Is what you wanted to know?"

"I don't suppose you know what the message said?" Marina asked.

Hari looked scandalized. "It was private message. Also, the envelope was sealed."

"I see."

As she was thinking they had probably found out all he knew, he spoke again. "The twisted man told me something to say to Baburao when I gave message."

He looked from Marina to Vijay, in obvious enjoyment of keeping them in suspense. At last he said, "I was to say to Baburao that he must not forget a rope can have teeth." He grinned. "When I have said this Baburao's eyes were very large."

The rope with teeth. Marina pushed her mouth into what she hoped was a smile and said, "Thanks."

Hari was standing, bowing over his palms. "I must go. Maybe someone wants to send messages." They said goodbye, and in a moment he rode past on his bicycle.

As her eyes followed Hari, Marina noticed two men standing across the street. One was smoking a cigarette and watching Hari ride away; the other was inspecting the gearbox of a black motorcycle. When Hari was out of sight the watcher spoke to his companion, and the two started across the street.

Marina touched Vijay's arm. "Those men have been following us," she said. "They were at Baburao's, and they were at the square before we went to the More house."

They stood up, and Vijay dropped money on the table. "They were on Palika Road, too," he said. "I saw them near the vegetable vendor."

A dirty curtain hung over a doorway at the back of the cafe. Marina and Vijay slipped behind it as the men reached the shop's entrance. A man in a pink turban looked up, startled, when she and Vijay came through the doorway into a little kitchen cubbyhole, but before he could speak they were out the back door. They were in a cobblestoned alley. One end was a cul-de-sac, the other led to a sharp turn. Marina thought she heard voices behind them. She and Vijay began to run.

Marina's sandals slipped on the stones and she fell against the wall, recovered her balance, and ran on.

Chickens squawked and fluttered in front of them. They needed to get back to the major streets, where there were people around, but doing that was bizarrely difficult. The spaces between buildings were so small that to squeeze into them would have meant immobilization, and each foul-smelling path seemed to lead only to another just like it. She looked back to see one of the men, bony and shaggy-haired, rounding the corner.

Running in this heat was like pushing through viscous liquid, every step in excruciating slow motion. Sweat dripped off her hair, flowed into her eyes and her ears, ran down her arms and the backs of her legs. Vijay's shirt, she saw, was clinging to his back, wet through.

They were in a passage where the backs of rickety buildings seemed almost to touch overhead. When they were halfway along it, a man leading a donkey turned a corner and started toward them. The donkey carried a load of wood that barely cleared the walls. The man and the donkey plodded forward. There was no way to get by them. Vijay halted and, unable to stop herself, Marina careened into him. They would have to turn back. Yet to turn back would be to run into the arms of their pursuers. The man and donkey continued, oblivious. They were so close that Marina could see how frayed the rope was around the donkey's neck.

She looked around wildly. There had been a tiny entryway a few steps behind them. She pulled Vijay back into it. The door into the building, she immediately discovered, was locked. The donkey lumbered along, neither he nor his owner looking at them. Now, she realized, he was between them and their pursuers. The men would not be able to get down the passage until the donkey left it.

153

"As soon as he passes," she hissed, and when the donkey's tail cleared the doorway they darted forward. As they reached the end of the passage she heard angry voices, and in a brief glimpse back saw the two men shouting at the donkey's owner. She and Vijay turned the corner and the sound faded.

Now they found larger streets easily. They were not, after all, far from the central square. All they had to do was get back to the car and driver and get out of Halapur.

They threaded their way through the late-afternoon crowds. The heat of the sidewalk baked through the soles of Marina's sandals and traveled up her aching legs. Ahead was the peepul tree. They had reached the edge of the square. Hari and his bicycle were gone, but the men still squatted in the shade and the women were gathered at the fountain. The car—the car wasn't where they had left it.

The driver must have moved it. Her eyes darted toward the side streets. It would be pulled up close by. Vijay, she saw, was looking around too. "Where is it?" she asked, nudged by panic.

"I told him—"

Marina felt breath on the back of her neck. "You are to come with us," a voice said. "I have a gun in my pocket."

The man who had spoken was the taller of the two who had pursued them, the one with longish shaggy hair. The other, shorter and stockier, stood close to Vijay.

Not knowing what else to do, she moved in the direction he indicated. I could yell. Surely they wouldn't shoot in front of so many witnesses. Maybe they wouldn't, but maybe they would. She tried to catch someone's eye—the *beedi*-seller on the pavement, the men who jogged by carrying a high-backed red velvet sofa—but life around the pump and the peepul tree continued in oblivious tranquility.

The men led Marina and Vijay into the same building she had seen them standing in front of with their motorcycle. The steps were stained with red splashes of betel juice, and a faded sign announced that inside could be found the "Everywhere Travel Bureau, Ltd." Marina glimpsed an uninhabited desk and a few brochures scattered in a wall rack before she was hurried up creaking wooden stairs to an airless corridor. The shaggy-haired man nodded at a door and the stocky man unlocked it. They pushed Marina and Vijay inside.

"You will stay here," the shaggy-haired man said, drawing a snub-nosed pistol out of his pocket. "One of us will be outside."

Marina found her voice. "How long?"

The man didn't answer. He and his companion left them, and she heard the key turn in the lock.


They were in a small room, its one window shuttered. The few wedges of molten glare that seeped around the edges of the shutters provided the only illumination. Two string cots sat in the middle of the otherwise bare floor. The heat was intense.

She dropped her bag and sat on one of the cots. "Nagarajan will kill us," she said. She lay down and closed her eyes.

Metal grated, and she heard Vijay say, "Shutter's locked." She didn't answer. She heard the cords of the other cot give as he lay down.

Her brain felt torpid with heat and hopelessness.

Pulling the scalding air into her lungs seemed like insane effort. She lay in a semitrance, unmoving.

"What happened to the driver?" she said, finally. She had meant to speak normally, but her voice was a faint rasp.

"They have tricked him, or paid him, or killed him." Vijay's words seemed to come from far away, or from underwater. Water. She tried to ignore the dryness in her throat. At the Taj last night she had ordered a fresh lime soda from room service—a tall glass half-filled with crushed ice and lime juice, and a bottle of soda water to mix with it. She had left, she remembered distinctly, half an inch of diluted liquid in the bottom of the glass. What would I do for that half-inch now, what money would I give, what acts would I perform. Only a short distance from here people are buying cool bottles of beer for a few rupees. The thought brought her close to tears.

She heard something—a chair?—being dragged down the corridor outside, and the voices of the men. "Can you understand what they're saying?"

Vijay's eyes were closed. "Something about an hour, two hours. Something about nightfall."

Marina forced herself to sit up, fighting off the black whirling in her head, the accompanying suggestion of nausea. "We have to get out of here," she said.

She surveyed the room. The window was the only possibility. She crossed to it. The rusty hasp and ring that secured the shutters were fastened with a new-looking steel padlock. She looked at the shutters and their rusting hinges. She remembered her screwdriver, her Swiss Army knife.

Scrabbling through her bag, pushing aside camera, wallet, her parcel from the Laxmi Emporium, she whispered hoarsely, "Let's look at the window again. I've got something—" The knife gleamed red in her palm as she showed it triumphantly to Vijay. The screwdriver was there, too, near the bottom. She pulled it out.

Vijay sat up. "My God," he whispered. "It would never occur to those chaps that a woman would carry such things."

The shutters were held in the window frame with corroded hinges. If one side could be loosened, they could open the window. If they couldn't get to the ground once the window was open, at least they could call for help.

There were three hinges on each side of the shutters. She wedged the knife under the head of one hinge pin and tried gently to pry it up. It didn't move, and showed no sign of looseness. She pushed harder but the pin, corroded in place, didn't give.

She chipped at the rust around the hinge, trying to clear the obstruction. After a few minutes Vijay took the screwdriver and went to work on another hinge. For a long time, she alternated chipping and prying without success. Her skirt and T-shirt were covered with flecks of rust, her hands orange-stained where perspiration had dissolved it.

At last, when she pried on the pin, she felt the slightest movement. "It's started," she whispered. Biting her bottom lip, she gently eased the pin up. It was turning, it was loose. Leaving it half loosened, she turned to the next.

The next two seemed easier, either because Marina and Vijay were elated by success or because the hinges were less rusty. Soon all were loosened.

Now to remove the pins and open the window. Carefully supporting the shutter, they took out the first two pins. At the instant Marina, her fingers trembling, extracted the third, the shutter, without warning, shifted its weight with a metallic groan.

They had time to do no more than exchange an agonized look before the key turned in the lock and the shaggy-haired man entered, his gun pointed at them. When he saw what they had done, he smirked. "Now you see the bars on the other side," he said.

It was true. The windows were barred. He took the knife and screwdriver and slid them into his pocket. Then he picked up Marina's bag and glanced through it, his eyes lighting up when he saw her camera. He slipped the camera in his pocket. My knife, my screwdriver, my camera. Three of my best tools gone.

He handed her the bag and motioned them to the door. Down the corridor, they stopped in front of another door. When he opened it, Marina saw that it opened into a closet. He removed a mop and a container of cleaning fluid and motioned them inside. He closed the door and once again they heard a key turn.

Now the heat, worse than in the room, was mixed with a harsh disinfectant smell. Her nausea returned, worse this time, and she steadied herself against the rough wooden wall. Vijay's hand closed over hers. She felt him slowly easing himself down to a sitting position on the floor, and she did the same. With their backs against the wall and knees bent they sat side by side, hands entwined.

Marina's eyes adjusted to the darkness and she could make out a rag hanging on a nail, light around the cracks where the door closed, Vijay's profile. Her mouth was drier than ever.

Gradually, thirst ceased to occupy her mind completely. Bright, vivid images bloomed in her head. She thought she saw Patrick, dressed in his white tie and tails, ready to conduct a concert. She had something to say to him, but she couldn't remember what it was, couldn't get her lips to move, couldn't speak because her throat had been burned in a fire. She tried to think of coolness. *Quench and revive the very one you have burnt up*. Quench and revive. Quench and revive. Something had been cool, cool on her neck, her burning throat. She tried to remember what it was. Something golden. Not Catherine's hair, something else. The necklace. Tiger-eyes.

She leaned toward Vijay and said, in the barest of whispers, "I have an idea."

This time the man outside the door must hear absolutely nothing. Very slowly, she let her hand fall to her bag and slid it inside the flap. Under her fingers she felt the parcel, wrapped in brown paper and tied with a string, that contained her purchases from the Laxmi Emporium. To keep the paper from rattling would be the first consideration. She began picking at the knot with her fingers. She must untie it. To try to break the string, or slide it off the package, would risk too much noise. She picked and picked at the string, unable to tell whether she was making progress or not.

When the knot finally loosened, she had to swallow convulsively several times before she could make her fingers remove the string. Next, fold by fold, muffling any sound by keeping the bag nearly closed, she opened the package.

Her hand slid on the silk of Clara's scarf and closed on the ornate handle of the letter opener. She discarded the tooled-leather sheath and felt the blade. It was not sharp at all, and the point was blunt. Maybe it could do some damage, though.

It wasn't enough. She and Vijay couldn't attack two men with guns armed only with a souvenir letter opener. She handed the letter opener to Vijay, who took out his handkerchief. Pushing down his sock, he tied the letter opener to his ankle with his handkerchief, then pulled his sock over it again. Maybe he had seen a superhero hide a stiletto that way in one of the films he liked so much.

Now for another weapon. She folded Clara's scarf to make a double-thickness square, then removed from the package, very carefully, the tigereye necklace. Even in this stifling atmosphere, the heavy stones were cool. Holding the necklace in the lap of her skirt, she tugged hard at the clasp.

As she noticed when she tried it on, the string was rotten. The clasp came away in her hands, and the loosened stones slid, with only the tiniest clinking, into her lap. One by one, muffling the sound, she placed them in the silk square and, bunching the silk at the top, tied it securely with the string that had been around the package. Holding the bundle by the excess silk and swinging the stones, she might be able to stun someone, if she took him by surprise. If it wasn't a surprise, there would be no chance at all. She replaced everything in her bag and closed the flap. She had done what she could. She reached for Vijay's hand and settled down to wait.

By the time the closet door opened to reveal the two men holding guns—shadowy now, in the dusk—Marina had imagined it so many times that the reality seemed just another mental run-through. She wasn't sure how long she and Vijay had sat there, breathing shallowly, close to blacking out. Two hours, perhaps. Two hours she wasn't sure she could have gotten through without Vijay's perspiring hand holding hers.

The shaggy-haired man hauled her to her feet. Her stiff legs would hardly support her when, moments later, she was led down the stairs. In the first humanitarian gesture they had shown, the men let first Marina and then Vijay use a filthy toilet behind the staircase. Gagging on the fetid air, Marina wondered what the cleaning fluid whose smell had choked her in the closet was used for.

She teased a trickle of water from the rusty tap, rinsed her hands, and gulped swallow after swallow from them. It seemed odd to remember how careful she had been to drink only bottled water. She finished by splashing her face. As the water evaporated in the evening air she began to feel slightly cooler. Her mind was very much on their makeshift weapons, but the men were obviously edgy and on guard, and there was no opportunity to use them.

When Vijay finished in the toilet the men led them out the back door of the building. A van, its rear doors open, was pulled up at the end of the alley. Beyond it, Marina could see the square, lit by mercury lamps. Smoke and the smell of cooking filled the air, and somewhere a radio was turned up to full volume. The shaggy-haired man motioned her into the back of the van, and Vijay climbed in beside her. Although there were seats under the side windows, the shaggy-haired man said, "The floor," and motioned to his stocky companion who pulled a length of thin cord from his pocket.

"No!" she cried involuntarily, but the stocky man ignored her and pulled her hands roughly behind her back and tied her wrists. If he bound their ankles too he was sure to discover the letter opener in Vijay's sock. After tying Vijay's wrists, however, he slammed the doors and joined the shaggy-haired man, who was already behind the wheel, in the front seat. The shaggy-haired man started the engine and the van pulled out.

Bumping through the streets on the floor of the van, Marina considered their options. The windows were closed, so crying out would be useless. The only possibility was to get the letter opener and use it to cut the cord around their wrists. At the moment, though, the van's interior was illuminated by the lights of Halapur, and the stocky man was looking back at them every few moments. Surely they would be leaving Halapur. If their destination were in town, why the elaborate arrangements with the van? And if they left Halapur, they would also leave the lights of Halapur. She braced herself against the seats, trying to counteract the jolts of the ride. The floor of the van was bare and uncomfortable. She wondered briefly whom the vehicle belonged to, and for what purpose it was used.

She looked at Vijay. His once-crisp white shirt was rumpled and smudged, his pants dust-streaked. Surely he and the car and driver would be missed in Bombay. Mr. Curtis would be worried. Vijay's parents would worry, too.

Mr. Curtis might not be worried, though—at least not yet. Since Vijay's involvement with her was strictly unofficial, Mr. Curtis might not want to know exactly what was going on. Also, Vijay had come on this trip in a defiant mood, with a trumped-up letter to mislead the police. Chances were he hadn't told anyone his plans. The consulate might assume, too, that the car and driver were with Vijay, wherever he was.

As for his parents—Vijay was twenty-five years old. It was possible that he stayed out all night from time to time with no questions. Even supposing everyone *was* worried, and everyone knew Marina and Vijay were in Halapur, well—they weren't, she realized, in Halapur any longer.

The last lights had gone by a few minutes ago, and the van was picking up speed. Silhouetted against the occasional illumination of oncoming traffic, the heads of their captors were turned forward. She waited. The glances the stocky man gave them were more widely spaced, and seemed cursory. Time to get started.

She edged toward Vijay. When he saw what she was doing, he positioned his leg closer to her tied hands. Every few moments, she stopped to make sure the heads in the front seat still faced forward. Thank God they had been made to sit on the floor, where they wouldn't be visible in the rearview mirror. She felt the wrinkled linen of Vijay's slacks under her fingers.

Finally, she found the hem of his pants leg and, when she pushed it up, the thin material of his sock. There was the knot of the handkerchief holding the letter opener in place beneath the sock. She wondered how much the stocky man could see if he looked back, and as if on cue his head turned. She froze, but he turned back after a brief glance.

No noise, no noise, she told herself as, pushing down Vijay's sock, she reached for the letter opener's handle and drew it from under the handkerchief. She maneuvered it so the blade was pointing straight out behind her.

She felt Vijay shifting his weight until his shoulder pressed her and she knew his wrists were near the blade. It took a few false starts, but soon they evolved a system. Marina, her feet braced, held the letter opener as steady as possible while Vijay rubbed the cord binding his wrists against it. Marina tried to remember exactly what the blade of the letter opener had felt like. It had not been nearly as sharp as the dullest knife, but it had had an edge. Subjected to the pressure long enough, the cord would fray and break. That was a physical law.

Things break because the stress placed on them is greater than the stress they are constructed to bear. The first rule of failure, the first step on the road to blame. Sitting in the back of the van, holding the letter opener while Vijay sawed against it, she thought, that's what my life has been for the last ten years—a long process of placing blame. Placing blame is my life's work, and why? So I can make sure no blame falls on me.

I believed that if I studied disasters long enough, and reduced them to numbers, and got to the principles behind them, I could prove conclusively that it wasn't my fault that Catherine died, that Agit More was killed. I still haven't proved it. I'll never be able to prove it. A tight place in her chest loosened a little. She redoubled her grip on the letter opener.

Some minutes later, the cord snapped. Vijay rocked backward when it happened, almost knocking the letter opener out of her hands. When he recovered his balance she felt him let out his breath in a long, soundless sigh and begin working his wrists loose from the cord. They must be far into the country by this time. The sky was black, and there seemed to be little traffic. The stocky man's head was drooping to one side. The floor of the van was almost completely dark. She felt Vijay flexing his fingers when the cord fell away.

The van slowed, then turned to the right. The stocky man's head straightened up and he looked around at them briefly. The new road was rougher. Marina wondered if Vijay would have time to loosen her bonds before they reached their destination. He took the letter opener from her fingers. The cord cut deeper into her wrists as he pulled at it, and she pressed her lips together to keep from crying out. The ordeal didn't last long. Working with both hands and the letter opener, Vijay soon broke the cord. She flexed her fingers and inched her arms forward to ease the muscle strain in her shoulders. As soon as she could move easily she reached into her bag and drew out the silk scarf tied around the tigereyes. It felt satisfyingly heavy in her hand.

The car was moving slowly because of the roughness of the road, but to incapacitate the driver meant risking a serious accident. On the other hand, to wait until the car stopped at its destination, where the men would be on their guard and there might be reinforcements, would be to wait too long. She could think of no way of getting the men to stop the car that would not make them suspicious.

All right. We risk a serious accident. Vijay still held the letter opener. The point was rounded and might not break the skin. She made a choking gesture and nodded toward the stocky man. Vijay nodded. Slowly, they rose to a crouch. She gripped the scarf and tried to estimate the distance. If the man turned now, he would see that they were free.

She took a breath, nodded to Vijay, and lunged at the shaggy-haired man, swinging the scarf with its burden of

165

tigereyes. It hit his temple with a solid crack and his hands loosened on the wheel. As she drew back to hit him again, she heard the stocky man's yell of pain and knew that Vijay had his arm around the man's neck. She brought the tigereyes crashing against the shaggy-haired man's temple again, and in the rear-view mirror saw his eyes go out of focus. He released the wheel and slumped toward the door.

Vijay and the stocky man were struggling. She brought the tigereyes down on the man's nose as the van left the road. He yelled again and brought his hands to his face, blood gushing through his fingers. The van, losing momentum, bounced through scrub and over rocks. It came to a sandy rise and plowed up it for a few yards, and the engine died. The headlights illuminated tumbled rock.

As they took his gun away, the stocky man groaned and muttered in a language Marina didn't understand. His shirt front was shiny with blood. The shaggy-haired man's eyelids danced as Marina searched his pockets, taking his gun and her camera, screwdriver, and knife. He would probably regain consciousness soon. They had to get away.

The van, sunk up to its hubcaps in sand, with liquid trickling from underneath it, was hopeless. They would have to go on foot.

They crossed the road, running. The moon had risen, indistinctly illuminating a landscape littered with boulders and scrub, without trees or shelter or signs of habitation. When at last they stopped to look back, the van's headlights were a tiny bright dot. The only sound was the rustle of scrub stirring briefly under a hot breeze. They went forward through the darkness.

They continued an hour or more without stopping, through prickly undergrowth that tore at Marina's bare legs, over rocks that bruised her sandaled feet. It seemed impossible that the sun would ever rise. Her body was swept by chills unrelated to the temperature of the night.

A rock-strewn hillside bulked in front of them. In the faint moonlight Marina saw at the top a tumbledown structure. "A hill fort," Vijay said. "We can rest there, perhaps."

Marina assented, realizing all at once that she could not possibly continue. She picked her way up the hillside behind Vijay. What might threaten her now? Dacoits? Snakes? Jackals? She didn't care about any of them. She cared about stopping, lying down. That was all.

The entrance to the fort was partly blocked by fallen stones. Beyond them the opening looked totally black. "You will stay here for a moment," said Vijay.

"Wait." She searched through her bag, found the flashlight, and held it out to him.

He took it with a dry laugh. "This bag you carry is full of miracles." She watched as, moonlight reflecting from his shirt, he climbed through the entrance and disappeared. At her last sight of him she wanted to cry out, to beg him not to leave her. She took the gun out of her bag and held it loosely at her side while she looked around, her scalp prickling.

There was a scrabbling sound, and several small animals darted over the pile of rocks at the entrance and disappeared into the undergrowth. Vijay appeared in the doorway and called softly, "You may come in now. It was rats only." She put the gun away and, shuddering, climbed over the pile of stones and into the ruined fortress.

It was not as dark as it had looked from the outside. Moonlight came in through holes in the roof. The room was solid and square, the walls thick, the floor uneven. Marina and Vijay sat down, leaning against the wall. After a moment she moved toward him and rested her head on his chest, letting herself be lulled by the rise and fall of his breathing, the thump of his heart.

Vijay's voice nibbled at her consciousness. "This is a good place. We are hidden. We must have water and food, but while it is dark we may pass water and food and not know it. Tomorrow we will continue."

"They might find us, when it's light."

"Possibly. Possibly not."

Sinking deeper into drowsiness, Marina said, "Vijay?"

"Yes."

"Why did you act so funny yesterday afternoon? This morning, too. Was it just that you were upset about your marriage?"

His chest filled, then slowly descended. "Not that only."

"Then what?"

"I did not like to hear that you had—been with this Nagarajan. It made me angry. With him and with you. Yet with myself, too, because what was it to do with me? I felt a great, tearing anger."

"It's all right now? Because if we die, I don't want to die thinking—"

His lips brushed her forehead. "It is all right. Do not think, anyway, that we shall die. We are warriors worthy of Shivaji himself."

Marina closed her eyes. With the next breath, she was asleep.

She awoke toward dawn, drenched with perspiration and racked with chills. Vijay's face swam above her. "You are ill, Marina?"

She nodded. He put a hand on her burning face and gave a hiss of concern. "I can walk," she said.

"I will come back in a moment," said Vijay, and before she could reply he was climbing through the doorway. She huddled against the wall, shaking uncontrollably. I am a warrior worthy of Shivaji himself, she thought in counterpoint to the list of diseases running through her mind: malaria, cholera, typhus, typhoid. Could she really walk? She pulled herself to her feet and took a few wavering steps. She could. Her skin was so sensitive that her hair brushing her neck, the sleeves of her T-shirt against her arms, felt as rough as sandpaper. She peered out the door.

The rising sun bathed the countryside in pink light, starkly picking out the rocky hills. No air stirred. Vijay stood a few yards away, shading his eyes. He turned and saw her and said, "I think I see what we must do." He pointed to a dark patch on the horizon. "There are trees. There will be water also, perhaps a farm or a village. If you can walk so far, we will go there."

And if I can't? "All right."

As they descended the hill, the first rays of sun flooded the landscape. She did not dare look at the dark blur that was their destination. She kept her eyes just a few yards ahead of where she was, willing herself to go at least that far. Her legs continued moving. The sun rose higher, its rays pouring on her head like hot liquid.

After a long time she stumbled, and Vijay said, "You would like to stop and rest?"

"I'm afraid to. I might not be able to start again." There was a bitter taste in her mouth.

"We will stop a moment." Vijay led her to the shadow of a boulder. When she sat down, the earth seemed to undulate, and she dug her fingers in the sandy soil to steady herself. She retched violently, her body heaving and producing nothing. Eventually the retching eased, and she sat still. She raised her eyes to Vijay's anxious face. "I love you, Vijay," she said.

"And I love you."

They continued, Vijay taking her bag and eventually supporting her with his arm around her shoulders. She forgot to look a few yards ahead and then was not conscious of looking at anything at all. She was aware of the blinding sun, a bitter taste, and Vijay. At some point he took off his shirt and draped it over her head, and put his handkerchief over his own. You'll burn, she wanted to say, looking at his smooth brown shoulders, his thin undershirt. You'll burn, you'll burn. "I'm burning," she whispered.

She saw Catherine. Are you dead or not, Marina demanded. Catherine smiled slowly, frighteningly, and melted into a pool from which a sleek, shining cobra emerged.

Something brushed her face, and she cried out. Looking up, she saw leaves. Her face had been brushed by leaves, leaves that dappled the sun on Vijay's shoulders. Down a slope she saw two women standing in a slow, muddy stream, their saris tucked up around their calves. The laundry they had been pounding on the flat, wet rocks hung in their hands as they looked up at her cry. She opened her mouth to say something, but her knees buckled and she whirled away.


The soft, rhythmic thumping had been going on a long time. It insinuated itself behind Marina's eyes, trying to force them open, but they did not want to open. The light behind her eyelids was a rich yellow-orange.

While listening to the thumping she became aware of an earthy, not-unpleasant smell of smoke, cut vegetation, cow dung. Soft voices exchanged a word or two. She tossed, momentarily frightened, and realized that she lay on a mat on the ground, under a rough coverlet. She remembered swallowing something hot with a strong taste, seeing firelight dance in the lenses of Vijay's glasses, feeling something cool pressed against her forehead.

She tossed again, and the thumping stopped. The voices spoke, and she heard rustling. She was able to open her eyes. Squinting, she found herself looking into the brown eyes and round dimpled face of a woman bending over her. Sunlight poured through a doorway behind the woman, illuminating another woman bent over a stone pestle. The thumping had been the women grinding grain. The light hurt Marina's eyes, and she closed them again and slept.

She awoke fully later, to the smell of hot oil and the sound of a small child wailing. Through the doorway, she could see that it was dusk. Outside, one of the women squatted next to an open hearth, feeding the fire. A toddler, crying, clutched at her sari. Marina raised herself on her elbow, looking around her at mud walls, rolled mats, round clay water jars, sacks containing, she supposed, some kind of grain. From outside came the lowing of animals and masculine voices. She wanted water.

A little girl holding a baby on her hip came and stood in the doorway. The baby gobbled at its fist as the girl came a step closer. Marina moved her mouth to say "Hello," but no sound emerged. The girl fled back outside, and Marina saw her whispering to the woman. The woman glanced toward Marina and then spoke to the girl in an authoritarian tone. In a few moments the girl was back, followed by Vijay.

Rumpled, barefoot, his hair uncombed, he looked completely different from the fastidious Bombay "minor functionary" who had introduced himself at the Hotel Rama. He knelt beside her and put his hand on her forehead. "The fever is gone. How do you feel?"

"Thirsty."

He left, and came back with water in a brass cup. "I have told them they must boil it for you," he said, giving it to her.

She drank and gave him back the cup. "I must have slept all day."

He smiled. "All day and another day. It was yesterday morning that we reached this place."

Yes, she remembered seeing firelight on Vijay's glasses. That must have been last night, and now it was almost night again. "What happened?"

"You have been ill, with high fever. The nearest doctor is half a day's ride by bullock cart. I wanted to go, but they said they would give something to you, and they made a medicine. I was worried for you to take it, but you were so bad I said to go ahead."

"Who are these people?"

172

"They are the family of Nathu Dada. They farm the bits of land that can be cultivated here. They own it themselves, which means they are better off than many small farmers. There is Nathu Dada, whose wife is dead, and two sons with their wives and children."

"What's the name of this place?"

"It has no name. We are far from cars or telephones. The closest village, Goti, is where the doctor is—half a day in the bullock cart, which is the only transport they have. For the next day or so they need the bullocks for farm work. We are what you would call stranded."

"Has anyone been looking for us?"

"Not yet. Surely, though, if those chaps who captured us are alive they or others like them will search. That worries me very much. I do not want these people to be hurt."

"Who did you tell them we are?"

"I said only that you were ill and we were in desperate trouble. You see, it is as it was at the house of Baburao. Our religion is full of stories of gods in disguise who knocked on doors and asked for help. The visitor, even unknown or unexpected, must be welcomed."

Feeling weak, Marina lay back. "What are we going to do?"

"You must recover. Can you eat something? I think you must try."

The dimpled woman brought her a bowl of cooked millet, and Marina scooped it up with her fingers. She was relieved not to feel her stomach heaving in rebellion. Later, she lay watching the firelight flicker while the family and Vijay ate their evening meal. Before they finished, she was asleep again.

The next two days passed as if lifted out of time, with

the heat, her unaccustomed weakness, and the strangeness of the circumstances adding to her sense of unreality. She bathed, dipping water out of a brass cauldron and spilling it over herself, and caught the dimpled woman, Gangabai, who was bold, friendly, and given to fits of giggling, peering at her with unabashed curiosity. I must look pale and ugly to her, Marina thought, looking at Gangabai's plump brown arms. They must think my short hair is awful, too. Marina had seen Gangabai and her sister-in-law, Shailibai, taking turns oiling each other's long black hair. When Marina had finished bathing and reached for her clothes, Gangabai, laughing, shook her head and Shailibai shyly offered her a sari instead.

Gangabai and Shailibai wore their saris tied up through their legs, but after several attempts to show Marina the method, punctuated by a great deal of laughter, they brought out another sari, petticoat, and blouse and showed her how to drape it in the way Marina was more accustomed to seeing. The sari was dark green cotton with an embroidered dark red border, the blouse embroidered in the same colors. When it was finally adjusted, Marina felt even more disoriented, as if she had become another person.

Gangabai and Shailibai seemed pleased with her appearance, but still not satisfied. They indicated her bare arms, her unpierced earlobes. Of course they'd think she needed bangles, earrings, necklaces. Her one necklace, the tigereyes, was still unstrung. They acted surprised when she spread her arms wide, trying to convey that she didn't have any. Gangabai went to a chest and came back with tinkling bangles of green glass, and Marina slid them on her arm.

Catherine had worn saris, cotton saris like this one. Catherine had known this feeling of the cloth brushing against her legs when she took a step, the fluttering when a slight breeze caught it.

Followed by the laughing women, Marina went outside to show Vijay. The compound was surrounded by a mango grove, which bordered the river. Not far away was the rutted track that led back to the world she knew. Soon she would have to think about all that again. Now, she would not think about it. It was as if the fever had burned away some keen edge of anxiety. Vijay was walking beside the river. When he saw her he ran to look, and he and the women and Marina, surrounded by children and Nathu Dada's old dog, exclaimed over Marina's new garments.

Vijay had offered to work with the men in the fields. Shocked, they had refused. "Why didn't they want you to help?" Marina asked.

He seemed uncomfortable. "It is this caste system. They think it would not be proper for me, a Brahmin, to work alongside them. I do not believe in these divisions."

"What would your mother think about your working in the fields?" she asked, and he smiled and turned away.

The two of them walked by the river and he talked about his conversations with the men. "They will not let me work with them, but they like that I tell them about Bombay."

"What do they think of it?"

"It is something they have not dreamed. I told them of the tall buildings, and they wished to know how those people living there could keep their bullocks up so high."

They walked far down the river, surrounded by trees, as the heat of the day dissipated, then sat on the bank in the evening quiet. A leaf traced a curling pattern in the air before coming to rest on Marina's knee. As she brushed it away, Vijay said, "Seeing you in a sari—it is very odd."

"Is it?"

"Yes. You will think I am foolish. It makes you more strange and more familiar at the same time."

Tenderness for Vijay welled through her, cool and delicate, washing over his black hair, his glasses, his stained clothes. She put her hand against his face and kissed him.

She felt his lips quicken. She had wanted to kiss Vijay for a long time, she realized. Her fingers traced the outline of his back.

"I have desired you so much," he whispered. "I knew it was stupid, stupid. Because how can—"

"Not stupid."

She hadn't expected to make love on the riverbank, half—but only half—hidden by trees, yet there was no point when it seemed right to stop. Tasting Vijay, caressing him, she felt lightheaded with joy. They laughed at their own eagerness, at the unsuitability of the terrain. "How wonderful that it's you, Vijay," Marina whispered, not knowing what she meant.

Afterward, as they watched the sun's last rays reflected in the river, playfulness and desire gave way to silence. Encircled by Vijay's arms, Marina thought, we don't speak of the future, because what can we say? Yet, when I believed I was dying, I told him I loved him.

The next day, when the men returned from the fields,

Marina saw them talking with Vijay. Later, as they walked along the river again, he held her and said, "I want you very much. It is difficult to wait, but if we wait until tomorrow night we shall have a place better than this."

"What do you mean?"

"The men have told me that tomorrow they go to the village, and they will take us there."

Marina's first reaction was dismay. To go to the village meant to go back to the world of danger, fear, murder— to go back to the problem of Nagarajan and the evil he had done, to go back to the problem of Catherine. "But why tomorrow?" she asked.

Vijay looked surprised. "You are not pleased?" He laughed. "You like the life of an Indian peasant woman?"

Feeling the blood rush to her face, she slid her arms around his waist. "Some of it has been very nice."

"So it has," he said softly. "However"—he assumed a mock-businesslike attitude—"Nathu Dada and his son will go to Goti tomorrow because they need to buy and sell at the market, and also because they have heard that Baladeva will be there."

"Baladeva? The dacoit?"

"Yes. For some of these peasant people he is a hero. He will hold darshan, something like a royal audience, and they will give him an offering. Possibly they hope this will remind him that he should rob the rich, and not their farm."

"If he comes out in the open, won't the police arrest him?"

"He will have his gang with him, well-armed. And who is to say the police do not admire and fear Baladeva

177

as well? I hope we shall avoid all that. There will be a telephone at Goti. The bus comes there too, and perhaps there will even be a car for hire.''

They would go back tomorrow. They would tell Mr. Curtis about Nagarajan, and about their abduction, and that would start an investigation. She would insist on knowing the truth. The river and Nathu Dada's farm already seemed distant.

The next morning started before dawn, with a flurry of preparations. Feeling badly rested and apprehensive, Marina dressed in Shailibai's sari. That she should wear the sari instead of her Western clothes had been Vijay's suggestion. "With this Baladeva about, it would be best not to call attention to yourself," he had said. "With the sari you will blend into the crowd more easily.''

In the cool half-light, she rolled up her T-shirt and skirt as small as she could and stuffed them in her shoulder bag. As she did so she saw the gun and the scarf with the tigereyes still tied in it—weapons she might need again, now.

At the first light, Nathu Dada, a taciturn, white-haired man, his round Gandhi cap on his head, clucked to the bullocks and the cart lurched forward as its massive wooden wheels began to turn. Sitting next to Vijay in the back, Marina waved to Gangabai and Shailibai, who stood on the baked earth of the front yard, children clustered around their legs. Gangabai's husband, too, was staying home. Shailibai's husband rode opposite Marina and Vijay, half-reclining on sacks of grain. As they moved away, the dog yipping behind, dust filmed Marina's view of the women, the house, the mango

178

grove. Only when all had shrunk into invisibility did she turn her face forward.

The journey was arduous—bone-rattling, dusty, and hot. Swaying in the back of the cart, the end of her sari shading her head from the sun, Marina gazed at mile after mile of tumbled rock. She wondered what had happened to their captors, the shaggy-haired man and the stocky man. Perhaps they had died in this waste, as she and Vijay could have died. She scanned the horizon. It was empty.

Toward noon, Nathu Dada stopped and, squatting in the shade at the side of the cart, they ate tortillalike bread made from millet that Vijay said was called *bagri bakar*. Soon after they resumed their journey, they began to see other travelers—people on foot or bicycle, bullock carts, a truck painted with bright designs whose rear-view mirror was hung with garlands of flowers. "Everyone is coming to see Baladeva," Vijay said.

In midafternoon, they approached Goti. The village was located in a curve of a slow, meandering river—the same one, Marina guessed, that flowed by the Nathu Dada farm. The cluster of huts and low buildings seemed alive with activity. Nathu Dada maneuvered the bullock cart to a stone temple, in front of which was the market—blankets spread on the ground, makeshift stalls selling batteries, plastic combs, oranges, guavas. A loudspeaker blared music. A sadhu, a wandering holy man, clad only in a loincloth and covered with ashes, crouched near the temple gate. After the quiet of the farm, the scene seemed feverishly alive.

At a corner of the market, Marina saw two flatbed trucks pulled up in front of a compound of huts surrounded by a low wall. Next to the wall a man wearing a loose-sleeved, thigh-length shirt and baggy cotton trousers, a rifle slung over his shoulder, was speaking into a walkie-talkie. A crowd milled about in the compound. She pointed and said, "Baladeva?"

"Yes, that will be where he is having darshan. If you ask the people there, they will tell you he never touches anyone who has less than ten lakhs of rupees, which means they are very rich. They will say he gives money to temples and to the poor, that he pays no attention to barriers of caste but treats all alike."

"Is it true?"

"I don't know. People have a great need to believe such things."

Nathu Dada and his son tied the bullocks, and Marina and Vijay climbed down from the cart. Nathu Dada accepted their expressions of gratitude with a grave nod, and in answer to Vijay's query pointed out the way to the police station.

When they found the office of the district police, however, it was locked and deserted. "I should have thought," said Vijay. "Of course they will not be here, with Baladeva in town. They will be patrolling far from here. We must find a telephone elsewhere."

A little farther down the street they came to a building slightly larger than the rest with a drooping flag hanging over the door. "This will be the office where the village administration is located," Vijay said. "Here there will be a telephone."

The office was manned by a clerk who seemed prepared to negotiate with Vijay indefinitely over the use of the telephone. Even after Vijay produced his identification, the clerk regarded his rumpled appearance with obvious scorn and, as Marina interpreted his demeanor, professed continued reluctance to let Vijay touch the old-fashioned black instrument at his elbow. After a final exchange in which Marina hoped Vijay had been insulting, the clerk placed the telephone within Vijay's reach and turned ostentatiously back to the papers on his desk.

There followed twenty minutes or so of Vijay trying to contact the operator without success, reaching someone and shouting to make himself heard, being cut off, and starting the process over again. Eventually he carried on an extended conversation and hung up.

"What did they say?" asked Marina.

"It was the operator only. I have asked to place the call to Bombay, and she says it will be perhaps an hour or two before the call can go through. She will ring back."

"An hour or two?"

He nodded. "I see you have not had much experience with our telephone system."

Marina felt let down, restless, and hungry. It had been a long time since their *bagri bakar* in the shade of the bullock cart. "Should we go out and get something to eat, and come back to wait for the call?"

"Better not. She says two hours, but she may call back in five minutes. It's impossible to know. We must simply wait."

They sat side by side on a bench. Marina watched the slowly turning ceiling fan. The clerk shuffled his papers, bustled out, and did not return. The telephone did not ring.

Finally, Marina said, "I'll go find something to eat and bring it back. You wait here for the call."

"Yes, go. But be careful, please."

"I will." She rested her face against his neck for a

moment. She could feel his blood beating, could taste the perspiration on his skin.

The market was busier than before. Marina bought oranges from a toothless old woman, then drifted on until she saw a man selling peanuts roasted in the shell. He measured them in a balance, then put them in a cone made from the page of a magazine and gave them to her. As she paid him, a flash of something bright caught the corner of her eye.

A woman across the market was adjusting her sari over her head, pushing back long yellow hair that had caught the sun. The woman's face was hidden. Her hand and arm were fair, her sari red and white.

"Catherine!" Marina cried, but her voice was lost in the babble of the market and the blare of the loudspeaker. The woman was moving away from Marina, weaving her way among the throng. Marina shoved after her, the peanuts she had just bought dribbling from their makeshift holder.

"Catherine!" she called again, but her throat had closed. The red-and-white sari moved farther away as a bullock, his tail lashing at flies, crossed Marina's path. When Marina caught sight of her again, the woman had just reached Baladeva's compound. The guard glanced at her and nodded. As the woman disappeared behind one of the huts, Marina pressed desperately forward.

The oranges she had bought rolled around Marina's feet as she pushed her way to the entrance of the compound. She could no longer see the woman in the red-and-white sari. At the gate a legless beggar sat on a flat cart and cried for alms. Beyond him, inside the compound, people stood in groups and children chased each other. A family of pigs rooted in a pile of rubbish.

As she hurried through the gate the guard with the walkie-talkie called out. She hesitated as he approached. "You've got to let me in!" she cried. "The woman who just came through here is my sister!"

The guard looked at her impassively. As she took a hopeful step forward he said, "Wait."

Seething with frustration, scanning the compound, she stood while he spoke into his walkie-talkie. He finished his conversation just as a wiry man with a camera hanging around his neck approached. Holding out an identification card the man said, "Chatterjee, *Journal of India*."

"What do you want here?" the guard said to the man.

"To speak with Baladeva."

"And why? All of you print nothing but lies. What is this camera? Baladeva does not allow himself to be photographed."

"My editor is prepared——"

Marina sped through the gate in the direction she had seen the woman take, around the side of the nearest hut. She found herself in an open area in the center of which was a hearth. A large pot over the fire filled the air with a pungent smell. More armed men. They lounged against the walls of the huts or lay on string cots scattered around the courtyard. Two stood guard outside a hut where the crowd—petitioners or offering-bearers, Marina assumed, waiting to see Baladeva—was largest. She did not see the red-and-white sari. The woman could be in any of the five or six huts scattered about the compound. She would have to search.

The huts were being used, apparently, as barracks for

Baladeva's gang. The first one she looked in was uninhabited, with clothing, bed mats, and boxes of ammunition strewn about carelessly. In the second a man and woman, both Indian, were energetically making love on a mat in the corner.

She ran to the third hut. A curtain hung over the door and from behind it voices, none of them feminine, drifted. She moved closer. Some of the conversation was muffled, as if people were speaking with their mouths full.

Cautiously, she pulled back the curtain. Several men were sitting around a communal bowl of curry, dipping into it with pieces of flat bread. She did not see the yellow-haired woman.

As she let the curtain fall, she felt a presence behind her. She turned and saw a man who looked around eighteen. A rifle was slung over his shoulder. Behind him, Marina saw the guard from the front gate hurrying toward them. "I'm looking for my sister," she said to the young man. He muttered something as the guard ran up to them.

"I have told you to wait!" the guard said angrily.

"I'm looking for my sister. She just came in here."

"Who are you?"

"My name is Marina Robinson, and—"

"You must wait when I say wait," said the guard. He took her bag from her shoulder and nodded at the younger man, who leveled his rifle at her. The guard searched through her bag, and with a feeling of dread she saw his hand emerge holding the gun she had taken from her shaggy-haired captor. Displaying it, he looked at her. "You enter Baladeva's camp against my order, with a weapon?"

"You don't understand—" she began.

"I understand well!" he roared.

Behind him, she thought she saw the woman in the red-and-white sari go past the door of a hut. "Catherine!" she called, but the woman didn't hesitate or turn, and in a moment she was hidden again.

The people waiting outside Baladeva's hut were looking at her, and a babble of disquiet swept the courtyard. "Who is paying you? The police?" demanded the guard.

Marina shook her head. Before she could say anything, the guard spoke with the younger man, who shoved her with his rifle butt toward the hut outside which Baladeva's petitioners were congregated. They crossed the threshold into a crowded room. Babies cried in women's arms, a shrunken old man regarded her with rheumy eyes, a group of chubby, prosperous-looking men stopped a discussion to stare. Near the door, sitting austerely upright, was Nathu Dada.

She nearly cried out at the sight of him, but stopped herself when she met his level gaze, which contained no sign of recognition. He could do nothing to help her, and if she called to him she might endanger him and his family. She looked away.

The next instant the man with the rifle prodded her forward across the room and through another door. They were in an enclosure stacked with clay jars, baskets, a rake, a wooden yoke, the large wooden wheel from a bullock cart. "I will see Baladeva," the guard said. He spoke rapidly to the younger man and went out the door.

Marina called, "Come back!" but he didn't return, and the slim fingers of the young man played nervously with his rifle. She would have to wait.

The room was obviously a storeroom. Its one small window was covered by a piece of sacking. There was no other door. She could hear the murmur of the group in the anteroom discussing, she supposed, her unexpected entrance. The young man guarding her looked as frightened as she was.

"I was looking for my sister. She's wearing a red-and-white sari," she said, but when she saw his hands tighten on his rifle she decided not to say anything else.

She sat on the dirt floor and rested her forehead on her bent knees. She had been unutterably, unforgivably stupid to follow the woman—Catherine?—yet the compulsion had been overwhelming. She would, she knew, do the same again. Even now, despite the trouble she was in, she felt prickles of excitement and apprehension at the thought that Catherine might be near. Baladeva might understand, if she explained it the right way. She tried to remember if any of the newspaper stories she'd read mentioned whether he spoke English.

By this time Vijay will be worried. I ran off without thinking about him, not once.

The guard was taking a long time to return. She tried to make patterns from the irregularities in the mud wall. Staring at the wheel from the bullock cart, she thought abruptly, unexpectedly, of Loopy Doop. The design was much the same—the wheel's spokes were like Loopy Doop's legs, reaching out from a central hub and traveling in a circle. For Loopy Doop, though, the ends of the spokes weren't connected into a wheel, but carried gondolas. One of the spokes had broken near the hub, and the gondola crashed into the ticket booth.

186

Marina looked intently at the wheel. A twig lay near her foot. She picked it up and on the dirt floor began to scratch a fault tree.

She hardly noticed her guard's apprehensive look as she drew the top rectangle, the Most Undesired Event. The Most Undesired Event was the breaking of Loopy Doop's leg. Under the rectangle, she drew a line and then half a bullet pointing up, the symbol of an Or gate. The Or gate meant that only one cause was required for the Most Undesired Event to happen, although there could have been more.

She felt hypnotized. Analysis of this kind had been, for a long time, her only release. She lapsed into it with a feeling of physical easing.

Now the tree branched into the possible causes for the leg's fracture. She drew another rectangle and labeled it DF, for Design Fault. Maybe Loopy Doop's design had too small a margin of safety, and didn't take into account mechanical stresses inherent in its operation. Not likely. Bobo had other amusement parks, other Loopy Doops. None of the others had had problems, and they'd been operating for years. She went on to another rectangle: Improper Operation. A lot of possibilities there. The ride could have been unbalanced, operated at too high a rate of speed, badly inspected and maintained. Her investigation had shown, though, that the ride hadn't been unbalanced, and the speed had been within safe limits. As for maintenance and inspection, the records had looked fine.

Her guard muttered something. She looked up and said, "I'm not doing anything. It's OK." One more aspect to think through. She drew a third rectangle and labeled it Material Defect. She stared at the MD

187

scratched in the dry earth. A material defect would mean that the steel had failed. That was where she'd gotten into trouble. She'd thought the steel was too soft, inferior, but that was because she'd blown the hardness test. The tensile and chemical tests hadn't borne her theory out.

According to this fault tree, nothing went wrong. Loopy Doop never broke.

She rubbed her forehead with her gritty hand. *It broke. And it's taken me this long, and I've come this far, to realize that somebody's lying. I spent all that time messing around with the numbers while somebody was pulling the strings.*

*So, who's lying, and about what? Design's out. That you couldn't cover up, in these circumstances. Operation? Possibly. Records can be faked. It's not unheard of.*

*Material. I convinced myself I was wrong on the hardness number, but what if I was right? What if I did the goddamned test right, and the other tests were wrong, or got screwed up somehow? Or somebody screwed them up. What if I jumped at the chance to be wrong?*

She put down the twig. *I may never get out of this, but if I make it back to California I'm going to do that test again.* "Sixty-five on the Rockwell B," she said to her guard.

He was shifting his weight from foot to foot. Brought back to the present, she realized that the atmosphere had changed. She heard male voices, speaking in tones of urgency. The crying babies, the buzz of conversation from the anteroom, had subsided. In a few minutes came the sound of running feet and shouts.

She stood up, her eyes meeting those of the young man. His Adam's apple bobbed. He went to the door and looked out, then called to someone.

The answer seemed to disturb him. He looked at Marina. "What is it?" she said, and he responded in his own language. She heard motors. Vehicles were pulling up in back of the hut. Keeping his rifle trained on her, the man looked out the window, then let the curtain drop and paced back to the door. Voices came from another room, then sounds of scuffling feet passing the door. Marina tried to see out, but the young man waved her back.

She wasn't familiar with the sound of gunfire, but she knew immediately that the series of staccato cracks she heard a second later could be nothing else. Then shouts and more shots. The man took her arm and pulled her toward the door.

She resisted instinctively, unwilling to go toward the firing, but he shouted at her and grasped her roughly, dragging her with him through the now-deserted anteroom. When they reached the entrance to the hut he peered out into the silent courtyard. After a moment he ran, pulling Marina after him.

They had gone only a few steps when Marina heard more cracks. Puffs of dust exploded near their feet. The young man's knees buckled, his hold on her loosened, and Marina saw the rifle slip to the ground. He fell on top of it, blood spurting from his neck. A bullet thumped into the wall beside her. She turned back to the shelter of the hut.

She heard more cries, and the shots seemed louder. She ran back into the storeroom and tore the sacking from the window.

The window was a small opening in the mud wall at a level a little lower than Marina's chin. Through it she saw one of the trucks that had been parked at the compound entrance pulling away. Its open bed was crowded, men with rifles leaning over the sides. In the split second before it rounded a clump of trees, she thought she saw the flutter of the red-and-white sari.

The other truck was parked outside the window, and men were running past to jump into it. Hoisting herself upward with all her strength, she managed to get her midsection onto the windowsill and, her head and shoulders outside now, pull again until she was sitting on it. Cursing her sari, she maneuvered her legs to the outside and dropped to the ground, buffeted by gang members running toward the truck. When one of them stumbled against her it caught the attention of another, who stopped to stare. She recognized the hostile face of the guard at the gate, who had left her to go speak with Baladeva.

His eyes were bloodshot, his face bathed in sweat. "It is you!" he cried. "You who are responsible for this!" He yelled something to his comrades, and she felt herself being pulled, by many hands, into the back of the truck, crushed by the bodies of the men. A few more jumped aboard, and as the truck pulled out she saw figures in khaki-colored uniforms rounding the side of the hut. The truck accelerated.

Through the uproar, she heard a voice calling her name. Shoving her way to the side, she saw Vijay running toward her, a few feet away. She also saw, in a crowd farther back, the white-haired figure of Nathu Dada.

"Vijay!" she screamed, and saw by the set of his body that he heard her. He had reached the side of the truck, and she was pushing to get a hand out to him, when one of the gang members hit him on the side of the head with a rifle butt. She saw his glasses fly off, saw him stagger and drop back and lie motionless. Then the truck rounded the trees, and he was lost from view.

Marina hardly felt the bodies jostling against her as the truck bounced over the rocky, unpaved track. She was only peripherally aware that the shooting had stopped, and that the men had subsided into grim, watchful silence. She gave way to grief for Vijay, seeing his anxious face as he ran, seeing him lie so still.

Nathu Dada did what he could after all, searched for Vijay and told him where I was. Vijay could be dead, he's certainly hurt, and it's my fault. I should make a fault tree of my life—every branch a mistake, every fork a wrong decision.

She was alone, caught in something she understood only vaguely, en route to a destination she could not imagine. Her bag, with the tools that had seen her through, with her passport and money and even her clothes, had been taken away. What remained? Her sandals and underwear and a cotton sari and blouse, now dust-streaked and filthy, that weren't even hers.

The men seemed to relax slightly now, and talked among themselves, although they still watched the road behind them closely. Aside from curious looks, they paid little attention to her. She had noticed the guard from the compound glaring at her, but even he made no aggressive move. She guessed it would be up to Baladeva, who must be in front of them in the other truck, to decide what to do about her.

They continued to climb, and the road narrowed. She tried to remember what she had read about Baladeva's gang. They camped in these hills, moving from place to place, sweeping down to carry out raids. The ease with which they got away and their increasing popularity among the poor were turning them into a political embarrassment. That must have been the reason for the police action today. Still, the attack could have been window-dressing. If the police were serious about capturing Baladeva they would follow, and there was no sign of them. She thought for the first time about the young man who had guarded her, remembered the blood spurting from his neck. That had been serious enough.

It was well after nightfall when the truck stopped. The road had become an all-but-impassable track. The headlights briefly illuminated the gray face of the rock they had pulled up behind, and the other, now-empty, truck. Then the lights went out and the darkness was almost total. Someone's hand jerked her to her feet as the men jumped to the ground. She jumped in her turn, still in a strong grip. When her eyes adjusted, she could see the dark forms of the men disappearing over the side of a hill, and could make out the face of the man holding her. As she had thought, it was the guard from the compound. The two of them followed the rest.

She could see no path, and the men had spread out through the rocks and scrub. She heard their running feet. Occasionally, the heavy sound of their breathing mingled in her ears with her own labored gasps. As they gradually descended there were trees, and plants with sharp spines that caught at her sari. The descent became steeper and the vegetation more dense, and eventually the group consolidated into single file to pass through a narrow opening between boulders. When Marina went through, she could just make out that she was in an open area where tents had been pitched. Aside from the occasional brief flicker of a flashlight, there was no illumination except the moon, high and silver in the starry black sky.

Figures hurried through the encampment, speaking in hushed voices. Marina's captor pulled her down behind a rock where he crouched with his rifle at the ready. Marina struggled to catch her breath. They're waiting to see if the police are coming, if they're going to be attacked. If they do come, I wonder if I can keep from being caught in the cross fire.

She wasn't sure what determined the moment when the danger of attack was considered to be past. People began walking around the encampment, a lantern was lit in one of the tents. Someone approached and handed Marina and the guard a cold chapati and an orange. Marina ate hers hungrily, watching the camp come cautiously to life. A few more lanterns were lit and hung in trees, and a small fire was teased into life.

Spitting out the last pits of her orange, Marina said to the guard, "I didn't want to hurt anybody. I saw a woman come into the compound. Do you know her? She has yellow hair, and she's wearing a red-and-white sari. Her name is Catherine."

The guard grunted. "It is for Baladeva to say. You have brought the police down on us like a herd of jackals."

"I didn't. I don't know why the police came."

"Our brother is dead because of you."

"If you hadn't made him guard me, he'd be alive."

"Baladeva will decide."

He stood and hauled her to her feet and led her through the dimly lit camp, past groups of men speaking in low tones, chewing on their cold bread. She noticed one of them, a bandage on his face, watching her closely.

They reached a tent in the center of the clearing, outside of which stood a tall man with a rifle. The guard left her under the tall man's surveillance and entered the tent. After some low conversation Marina heard a voice say, in lilting, musical English, "Yes, yes, you must bring her to me now. Immediately."

No use to run. Her eyes met those of the stocky man, a bandage over his nose where she had broken it, and she saw the look of triumph on his face. The next moment, she was entering the tent.


Light from a swaying lantern cast increasing and diminishing shadows of Marina and the guard on the side of the tent. It played on the barefoot man in the long, loose, V-necked shirt and pajama-style trousers who sat cross-legged on a rug richly pattened in blue and gold. When he saw Marina, he placed his palms together and bent low over them. There was mockery, Marina thought, in the depth of his bow.

Nagarajan's once-luxuriant hair was roughly clipped close to his head. Without it and his flowing robes, and with the moustache that now shadowed his upper lip, his aspect was more conventionally masculine than when she had known him before. His face, with its dark eyes and exquisite bone structure, showed no sign of the passage of ten years. Just above the neck of his shirt, she saw the scar. He spoke briefly to the guard, and the man withdrew.

He gestured for her to sit on the rug in front of him, and she lowered herself slowly. When they faced one another she saw the amused smile she remembered.

"You have reached me after all, Marina," he said. "I would have thought it simpler to come directly from Halapur with the men I sent to fetch you. Now I recall that the simple way never appealed to you."

"Where is Catherine, Nagarajan?" How often had they played this scene? Had nothing changed at all?

"Please to call me Baladeva now. In India, you know, we believe in many incarnations, many lifetimes. Nagarajan was another life. But you do not know, do you, that Baladeva is also the name of a *nagarajan*. Taking that name was a tiny game I played."

"And Catherine?"

"It is strange how things do not change." He knew, she felt, that he was echoing her own thought. "When you came to see me first, it was to search for Catherine. Now you have come again, and still you search for her."

"Where is she?"

"She is dead, as you know, yet she has led you to me. It is a paradox. How can the dead lead the living? Yet you have followed her all these years, and not the last days only."

"You say she's dead. I got a letter, a phone call."

"What are those? Words on paper, a voice in the air. They have significance only when mingled with your own need."

"I saw her come into the compound."

"Suppose you see a white dove fluttering in a trap in the top of a tree. When you look again closely, it is a white cloth caught on a branch, blown by the wind. The dove is not real, you will say, but was it not real in some sense when you saw it? You must ask yourself, more important, why out of harmless cloth you have created a struggling bird."

Perspiration stood on Marina's forehead. "Where is Catherine?"

"Have you not understood? Catherine is with you. Nowhere else, except in the dust of Halapur."

She could see nothing but Nagarajan's bland, unreadable eyes. "There is a woman who has yellow hair and who wears a sari. I didn't imagine that."

"No, you did not." He called, and the man outside the tent looked in. Nagarajan spoke to him, and the man replied and left. "We must wait a short while," he said.

Nagarajan uncrossed his legs and reclined on the rug, leaning on one elbow. The gesture made Marina's breath catch. "Baladeva," she said. "You got out of jail and became Baladeva. How did you convince Joginder and Baburao to help you?"

His lips curled. "Joginder was frightened out of his wits, and more than ready to get me out of Halapur or do anything else I asked. Convincing Baburao let me out of jail was a matter of even greater simplicity. More than anything, Baburao wanted to own a field. I offered him the chance to have what he wanted, which is what I have always offered those who come to me."

"Whose body was cremated?"

"A homeless wanderer who slept on the sidewalk near the prison."

"You killed him?"

"I? Locked in a cell, how could I kill him? Baburao brought him in and gave him something to drink, and when his eyes became heavy Baburao twisted the cord around his neck."

"All for a field."

"It made him happy, I believe."

"Until you had him summoned to that field in the middle of the night and killed."

"You accuse me, I see. Yet had you yourself not thrown us out of balance Baburao would still be alive."

Marina shook her head. "You threw things out of balance when you sent those letters and had someone call me from the Rama. That's what made me think Catherine was alive, and put me on your trail."

He raised his eyebrows. "Undoubtedly those things put you on my trail, but if you think I was behind them you are mistaken. I sent no letters. I knew about the call because Raki, one of the few people who knows of my former life, told me after it happened. I assure you I had nothing to do with it.

"Consider, Marina"—he held up a forefinger— "Nagarajan has been cast away, like a snake's old skin. Baladeva is strong, and loved, and famous. Do you realize how powerful I am now?" His face was radiant.

"Is Elephanta Trading and Tours a front for moving what you steal?"

"It is clever, is it not? Boats come to Elephanta from the opposite coast, and from there go to Bombay. I myself go sometimes. I move freely in Bombay because I have many, many friends there. What I am saying, however, is this: The elements of my past life are of no more use to me than a snake's old skin is of use to him."

She wondered if he was lying. "If you didn't do it, who did?"

He shrugged. "For the answer, you must search your own mind. Certainly I would not disturb you with letters and calls about your sister. When I learned you were here, I wanted to avoid you. Failing that, I wanted to

197

capture you. I could do neither. Only your own utter determination, which I remember quite well from before, has brought you here."

It made a weird sort of sense. As a guru, Nagarajan sought power, wanted to have people in his grasp. As a dacoit, he wants the same thing. He may have shed his skin, but the essence is unchanged.

"It's too bad these men you lead don't know what you really are," she said.

"Do *you* know what I really am, Marina?"

Voices came from outside. A woman in a red-and-white sari entered, knelt, and touched her forehead to Nagarajan's feet. She straightened and looked at Marina.

Her yellow hair, thick and shining, fell past her shoulders, framing a long, serious face sprinkled with freckles. Her lips were thin, her eyes light brown. *I want always around me women with hair the color of mustard blossoms*. The woman regarded Marina without expression, but when her gaze shifted to Nagarajan Marina recognized the adoration of the devotee.

"Sylvie came here from Paris to write about me for a magazine," Nagarajan said.

Catherine had been taller, blue-eyed, bigger-boned. Sylvie didn't look any more or any less like Catherine than a cloth fluttering in a tree resembles a struggling dove. Marina bent her head, and felt the air stir slightly as the woman left.

"She became convinced that we represent a genuine movement of the people, and she has dedicated herself to our cause." Satisfaction was evident in Nagarajan's voice.

Catherine was dead, mixed with the dust of Halapur

for ten years. Tears slid down Marina's cheeks and dropped into the pattern of the carpet. *She is with you, nowhere else*. She had found Catherine after all.

After a while, Nagarajan stirred. His voice pulled her back to awareness of her surroundings. "There is an expression, is there not, that one who has died has 'gone before'?" he said. "Catherine has gone before, and you have followed her to this point. Now, you must join her where she is."

He couldn't let her live. She was part of the skin he had cast off, and she must be cast off as well.

"You'll sacrifice me the way you sacrificed Agit More," she said.

He took a pistol and holster from a pack in the corner of the tent and strapped them around his waist. Over his shirt he slipped a sleeveless vest long enough to cover them. "You have misunderstood the case of Agit More," he said. "It was a sacrifice, the holiest of acts. To kill you is a necessary act, not a holy one. For a sacrifice, the victim must be a boy, unblemished, never a woman or an enemy. Catherine understood this, as did the other two who assisted me in the ritual."

*Everything I feared most is true*. She felt herself to be in a place that was open, featureless, colorless, breathing something more refined than air.

"As far as my men are concerned, you are a police informer who entered our compound in Goti with a weapon," Nagarajan said. "They will not question what happens to you. It will be best, if they do not know too much. I think you will simply come with me."

She stood. Nagarajan motioned toward the entrance of the tent, and she started on her last walk with him.

The silent stares of the men Marina and Nagarajan passed as they left the camp were almost tangible—cold, impenetrable, unyielding. She saw the shaggy-haired man she'd hit with the tigereyes. He scowled and muttered something. Sylvie stood impassively in the shadows. They'll watch me go to my death. They'll do that because it's what Nagarajan—Baladeva—wants.

Nagarajan's face was solemn. His hand was gentle on her arm, almost as if he touched her only to keep her from stumbling.

When they left the camp and passed a patrolling sentry, Nagarajan took the pistol from his belt and pressed it against her side. "You will walk ahead of me slowly. We will not go far."

She took a step. "Nagarajan?"

"Yes?"

"Don't shoot me without warning. Let me know when, all right?" She didn't know why this was important, only that it was.

"Yes, yes. Walk on."

They wound over a rough path through precipitous terrain. These are vultures here, Marina thought. She remembered the tour of Bombay she had taken the day Agit More was murdered. The bus passed by the Parsee Towers of Silence and the guide told how, with solemn ceremonies, dead bodies of the faithful were placed there for the birds to clean. When no flesh was left, the bones were disintegrated with chemicals.

My bones will tumble and splinter among these rocks. Her mouth tasted of salt. The grit beneath her eyelids, the itching in the palm of her hand, the stones in the path seemed infinitely precious. She breathed and smelled her own body, and Nagarajan's, and a hint of smoke from the camp, and a dry aroma of dirt and vegetation that was the earth. *Catherine is dead but I'm not.*

"This is far enough." Nagarajan turned to face her. They stood by the rocky, sloping side of a gully that seemed, in the darkness, to have no bottom. Nagarajan's eyes reflected moonlight. The pistol, in his right hand, was by his side.

He drew her to him as if for an embrace, and, holding her tightly, placed the gun against her temple.

"You'll really kill me, Nagarajan?" she whispered.

His arm tightened. "You have been a great bother to me, although you gave me much pleasure also."

*Much pleasure.* She remembered their nights together in the ashram. She reached toward his face, not knowing why exactly, perhaps in supplication, and realized in midgesture what she must do. She stroked the scar, the mottled scar at the base of his throat.

His right hand, as she knew it would, as it always had, moved to brush hers away. In that reflexive instant she jerked herself to one side and wrested the gun from his momentarily loosened fingers.

After a split second of paralyzed shock, she ran beyond his reach and pointed the gun at him. Her finger tightened on the trigger. He turned toward her, the moon full on his face. He looked surprised but also, she would have sworn, admiring.

He started toward her. She pulled the trigger and saw his teeth flash in what was either a grimace or a grin as he dodged into the gully. When the shot stopped reverberating in her ears she heard the crackling underbrush and sliding gravel of his flight. Standing on the gully's edge, she fired toward the sound. She had no idea if she had hit him. When the scrambling noises faded she stood, clutching the gun, not believing that she was alive.

If he wasn't hit he would be back, but surely he would first go to the camp for another gun, and perhaps reinforcements. She ran frenziedly, then crouched, panting, in a sheltering crevice of rock to catch her breath.

The first shots had about the same volume and rhythm as the sound of a woodpecker pecking a tree. She shrank back against the rock in terror, certain, even though they were far away, that they were somehow directed at her. She strained to hear. The noise remained distant. Then she understood that the police had attacked the encampment after all.

Comprehension brought her to her feet. She started toward the noise. If she could find the police, she could get away.

As the firing got louder she could hear shouts as well, and see an unearthly glare. She gripped the gun more tightly and slipped from rock to rock in the increasingly illuminated landscape. Amid a confusion of shouts, groans, and cries, the firing stopped. On a rise ahead, she saw running figures silhouetted against the light, which she realized must come from searchlights the police had trained on the camp. Through the babble, she heard a motor and saw, off to one side, a jeep pull up next to a patch of scrub. A man vaulted out of it and paused to light a cigarette. The light of the match glared briefly on his open khaki shirt, his pudgy face and hands. He stared at her, startled, and then she realized that the shrill voice calling for help had been her own.

\* \* \*

The surprised policeman, who told her his name was Sergeant Aziz, placed her in the front seat of his jeep after gingerly taking her gun away. "We have heard of the missing American lady," he said. "It is lucky you were not with these dacoits. They were determined to fight, and now they had the worst of it."

"Who reported that I was missing?"

"The American consulate in Bombay, first. Then the driver of the consulate car, who was lured away from his post by some of these dacoits and given false information that he was to meet you at another place."

"I was with an employee of the consulate. Do you know—"

"Mr. Vijay Pandit was injured earlier today. He is in hospital but I think is not seriously hurt."

Tears of relief welled in her eyes. The policeman sketched a salute, said, "I must leave you, miss," and dashed toward the light and noise. Marina sagged against the lumpy seat of the jeep.

She stared for a while at the shadowy play of figures moving back and forth. Then she got out of the jeep and walked shakily to the edge of the ravine. She had to see.

Below, bleached and unreal in the bright light, was the confusion of the police mopping-up operation. Men in khaki picked their way around fallen tents and kicked overturned cooking pots. Others herded prisoners, tied together with rope, toward a waiting truck. One of the dacoits shouted something in an anguished, angry voice, and a policeman hit him a solid blow with his fist. When the man regained his balance, the policeman hit him again.

Marina's eyes were drawn to a row of bodies, ten or so, laid out like game after a day's hunt. Nagarajan was among them. The front of his shirt was stained dark red, his legs flung wide apart. So I got him.

"You must move back, miss!" Sergeant Aziz cried, and she obediently turned toward the jeep. He hovered near her, as if afraid she would make some other unexpected move.

"The leader of the dacoits—Baladeva," she said. "He was killed, wasn't he?"

"He is dead. We found him at the edge of the camp. It is an odd thing. He was covered with blood, as if he had been wounded and run a long way, yet he was at the edge of the camp only."

She had shot him, and he made it back to camp only to collapse and die as the police opened fire. It was an irony he would have appreciated. She sat in the jeep with her head on her knees, her mind blank.

When Sergeant Aziz returned, he was carrying something. He handed it to her. "This is yours, I think. We found it in one of the tents."

She took her canvas shoulder bag. Everything was in it—her clothes, her tools, her passport, even the tiger-eyes in the silk scarf. All seemed foreign, unimportant. She closed the bag and put it at her feet.

At last, Sergeant Aziz and several other policemen got into the jeep with her and the driver started the motor. The searchlights had been turned off. The area was as dark and featureless as when she had first seen it. The moon was setting. She turned her face toward the breeze stirred by the jeep's motion.

She dozed, her mind filled with images as jerky and speeded-up as an old movie. She saw Nagarajan in his robes, his long hair flowing, and in his other incarnation as Baladeva. She saw Patrick and Vijay, and Clara and Agit More. All of them, Nagarajan and Baladeva too, were dancing a jumpy little dance together. Catherine joined the dance, and an unconsciousness descended from which Marina awoke when the sky was gray with dawn and the jeep was pulling up in front of a hotel just off the main square in Halapur.

Sergeant Aziz escorted her inside, rang the bell insistently, and booked a room from the sleepy clerk who emerged from the back. "We shall wish to talk with you later, but I think you must rest first," he said. "This afternoon I shall call for you."

The room was plain, but clean. The ceiling fan stirred thin curtains through which came the light of daybreak. She took off the green sari and folded it carefully, then stood in the uncurtained shower letting hot water stream over her face, her hair, her body, stinging the scratches and cuts on her legs and feet. Scrubbed clean, she lay in her bed, watching the fan and listening to the sounds of Halapur starting the day. The room was bright with the sun's first rays before she fell asleep.

When she was awakened, by a soft, insistent knocking, the room was flooded with noon light. Thinking she would tell Sergeant Aziz she wasn't dressed and ask him to wait outside, she wrapped herself in the printed cotton coverlet from the bed and opened the door a crack. Standing there, holding a tray with a teapot and two mugs, was Vijay.

He looked worn and tired, and his glasses frames were held together on one side by white adhesive tape. He was smiling, though, his hair was neatly brushed, and his white shirt and beige linen pants were freshly laundered.

He again resembled the crisp, dapper young man who had, only days ago, called on her at the Hotel Rama and waited decorously outside the door of her room.

He did not hesitate today. When she flung the door open he walked in, put the tray on the foot of the bed, and put his arms around her. "I was afraid you were dead," she said.

"I wanted to be dead, because you were taken away."

"Vijay. Baladeva was Nagarajan. I killed him." Tears flowed down her cheeks, dripping off her chin and wetting the bedspread she still clutched around her.

He held her shaking shoulders tightly. "It cannot be true."

"It is."

They sat on the bed and she told him everything.

When she finished, his face was grave. "He would have killed you, because you knew his true identity."

*Do you know who I really am, Marina?* "He said he didn't make the call or send the letters, but he might have been lying."

They lapsed into silence. After a moment or two, she felt Vijay's fingers lightly tracing the line of her backbone, felt his lips against the back of her neck. Warmth slid through her. She said, "I'm supposed to meet Sergeant Aziz. He'll be here any minute."

"He won't," Vijay murmured. "I have spoken with him myself this morning, when I was released from hospital. He is most busy with the dacoits who were captured last night. It will be more convenient for him if I bring you along to the station later, as I have offered to do."

She turned to him gladly. *I didn't die. I'm alive after all.*

206

Later, as they lay entangled in the cotton coverlet, she said, "What about Mr. Curtis?"

"Mr. Curtis, you may imagine, is not pleased." Vijay's drowsy voice had an edge of discomfort. "I have spoken with him this morning. With my father and mother also."

"Are your parents terribly upset?"

Vijay wriggled as if bothered by an insect. "Terribly," he said, sounding more awake. "I am the youngest. They act as if I were still a child only. I had to beg my mother not to come here to Halapur to care for me."

"They've been frightened."

Vijay sighed. "Yes, yes."

Marina raised herself on an elbow and gazed at Vijay's face. "Is everything all right? You aren't going to lose your job, are you?"

He frowned. "As I said, I have talked with my father and Mr. Curtis. They have also talked with each other. They agree that for the most part I could not have helped what happened, but Mr. Curtis feels that in some areas I overstepped. They have met at the club for a chat and decided that I shall be given another chance." Vijay turned his face away from her.

Marian thought she understood. "You'll be given another chance under what condition?"

"Condition?" He still refused to look at her.

She turned his face to hers. "You can keep your job and make your parents happy if you marry Sushila and settle down. Isn't that it?"

His answer was the unhappiness in his face. Finally, he burst out, "Why can I not live as I please? I want to be with you, Marina!"

"You're with me now," she said, and he reached out to her.

# California

## THE FAULT TREE

The person constructing a fault tree must have a complete grasp of the system under scrutiny. If the complexities of the system aren't totally understood, the fault tree will be meaningless.

*Why Breakdown?*

THE BATHROOM MIRROR IN HER APARTMENT told Marina that her face was still peeling from sunburn. She looked drawn, too, but the relaxation, the near-torpor, of her last days in India had taken away the worst of the physical strain. Her sessions with the police and with Mr. Curtis had not been taxing. The police were more than willing to take credit for the discovery that Baladeva was Nagarajan, and for his death. Her part in the subsequent uproar was minimal.

Indian reaction to the events had been shock and outrage, but the reasons for the shock and outrage varied. People were shocked and outraged that the police had killed Baladeva, or that Baladeva had turned out to be Nagarajan, or that Nagarajan had escaped from jail in the first place. A commission of inquiry was being established. Government ministers gave assurances that everything possible would be done to bring the facts to light. In the meantime, Marina refused to speak with the press and lay by the pool at the Taj eating hot, freshly roasted cashew nuts.

She and Vijay spent languid, sadness-tinged evenings together with less and less to say to each other. They did not speak of her imminent departure or his upcoming marriage. Marina had been willing to slide from one moment to the next without much thought. She ate, slept, told her story when official inquiry demanded, made love with Vijay, read the newspapers.

One afternoon she summoned the energy to call the Delightful Novelty Company and ask for Vincent Shah, the man who had placed the call to her from the Hotel Rama. Mr. Shah was away for a week, the secretary said. The telephone receiver was heavy in Marina's hand. She should pursue this, insist on getting in touch with Vincent Shah. She hung up and lay down for a nap.

Eventually, the word came that she could go. She made a plane reservation and packed her suitcase.

Her plane left at six in the morning. She and Vijay drank milky tea from the stall in the airport, surrounded by the hubbub of transit—wailing children, quarreling porters, unintelligible announcements over the public address system. When it was time for her to leave, he said, "I will not embrace you."

"It isn't the custom."

"You know very well that my love goes with you."

"And mine stays with you."

Leaving him, she moved into the stream of travelers toward the plane that would take her home.

She dressed slowly, still easing herself back into her San Francisco life. Her sweater felt scratchy, her boots heavier and more cumbersome than they'd seemed before. In the two days since her return she had cried a lot—not only at the news that Clara had entered a hospital, but at Patrick's copy of *The Gramophone* lying on a table, and a box of cereal sitting where she'd left it in the kitchen, and the downtown high rises glistening against the sun-washed sky. She recognized this emotional fragility as temporary. I lost something. Now, I have to figure out what's next.

When she stepped outside, the morning air was chilly, astringent, but with the slight softness of early March, and yellow flowers nodded on the bush by the front door of her building. Flowers as yellow as mustard blossoms. A pollen-dusted bee crawled out of one and flew away.

By the time she reached the waterfront the fog had started to burn off and the bay was glimmering in the emerging sun. When she walked into the office one of her coworkers, hurrying past, said, "Hi, Marina. How was vacation?"

Don did a mock double take when he saw her and said, "What a tan! You lost weight, too."

"I might as well have gone to a health spa."

"We got your telex. There was a little something in the papers here, too. Listen, Sandy wants to see you instantly."

Sandy's face sagged and his eyes were bloodshot. She

had the feeling that his questions were perfunctory. "I'm sorry about your sister. It's like losing her twice," he said.

"In a way it's a relief." I won't be looking for Catherine again.

Sandy picked up a bulging folder. "I'm gald you're back, because we've got a ton of work. Since I took over Loopy Doop a lot of other stuff has had to slide."

"Speaking of Loopy Doop—"

"OK. Let's speak about it." He put the folder down. "I appreciate that you were under stress, but you left the case. I hope you don't have any idea of picking it up again."

Why the defensive tone? "It's just that while I was in India I thought about it, and I wondered—"

"The case is finished. We're working on the final report now. Frankly, I don't want you dividing your attention."

She realized for the first time that on some level he had been furious that she had left him in the lurch. "I'd like to know how it came out, then."

Sandy, his jaw set, didn't reply.

"Won't you even tell me what you found?"

He sighed. She wondered if he was just angry, or if something else was bothering him too. "I'll give you five minutes on it, and that's it. Agreed?"

"Agreed."

"It got very sticky. The short version is, the mainte-nance guys blew it bad, and then faked records to cover up." He stopped. "Why are you shaking your head?"

She hadn't realized she was. She remembered the maintenance chief with his tobacco wheeze and his terror of being blamed. He had sworn the inspections were in order. "How did you find out?"

"The forms they recorded the maintenance routine on."

"But they were all perfect. I looked through them myself."

"Absolutely. Only all of those perfect records were done on forms that weren't even in use until the week before Loopy Doop went smash. The only way to tell was a number in the corner. All those checks in the little boxes were made after the accident and stuck in the files to make it look like the inspections had been done."

Stunned, she started to shake her head again, then caught herself. "How did you find out?"

"One of the Fun World secretaries noticed the forms and told Jack Sondergard."

"What does the maintenance chief say?"

"Screams he didn't do it, he's being framed, but don't they always?"

Marina started to ask why, if the maintenance chief had known he might be vulnerable, he had called Breakdown in the first place. He had been proud, she remembered, that he hadn't waited for authorization. Instead, she said, "What broke the leg, then?"

"We're postulating excessive vibration because it was improperly lubricated."

"Postulating? What did the hub and shaft look like? And the bearings?"

Sandy's eyes were averted. "That was the other thing," he said.

"The other thing?"

"Right after you left, Bobo ordered every Loopy Doop in the country dismantled and melted down for scrap. By the time we came up with this theory—"

212

"There was nothing to look at."

She couldn't argue. With Loopy Doop destroyed, there was no possible proof. When the maintenance chief had wheezed about how well he'd done his job she'd told herself that he would probably be trotted out to take the blame.

Sandy shrugged. "I guess Bobo wants to forget Loopy Doop ever existed."

"Yeah." She was having trouble taking this in.

"So that's that." Sandy reached for the folder.

Forty-five minutes later she put the folder on her own desk and dropped into her chair.

At a time when she had been in desperate danger, she had scratched a fault tree in the dirt. She had decided somebody was lying in the Loopy Doop case. Sandy was saying she was right. The maintenance chief had lied and covered up. Why, then, did she feel dissatisfied?

Because of the damn hardness test. Sandy's explanation still meant that she had messed up the hardness test. In Goti, she had realized she didn't have to assume she was always wrong, that maybe once in a while she was right.

She opened the folder. There was a lot to do, and she'd better get started. With this much to occupy her, it wouldn't surprise anybody if she decided to work late tonight.


Staring at the screen of her computer terminal, Marina jumped when something touched her shoulder.

"Didn't mean to scare you," Sandy said. He patted her shoulder again. "Quitting time."

"When I finish this. Not much more to do."

"Listen. I wasn't as nice about the Loopy Doop thing as I could've been. I'm sorry."

No matter how much he apologizes, I'm going to redo the hardness test. "Don't worry about it."

"I've had a lot on my mind."

"Sure." She glanced at him. "Where's Don?"

"He left already." He hesitated. "Don and I aren't exactly together any more."

So that was it. "That's too bad."

"Oh, hell, it happens all the time. I don't guess either of us thought it was till death us do part." Sandy's laugh sounded thin. "See you tomorrow."

After another half hour the pier was completely quiet. When she left her cubicle she waved across the interior to Fernando, the security guard, sitting at his table beside the door, his uniform cap perched on the back of his head. Her steps sounded loud in her ears, and she felt more nervous than she had expected. I'm doing this for my own satisfaction. If I did the test wrong, I'll live with it. I want to see, that's all. Tension traveled up her spine.

She slipped the key to the evidence room out of its magnetized box. This isn't wrong. Unauthorized, maybe. Against orders. Not wrong. Redoing a legitimate test isn't wrong.

The evidence room was dark, but she remembered where she'd put the fractured tubing. When her hand didn't find it she turned on the light and surveyed the tiers of bins. In the bin where she'd put Loopy Doop's leg, there was now a yellow molded-plastic automobile infant seat.

It had been moved. OK. She searched systematically through the bins. Now that finding it was more difficult than she'd expected, she was more determined.

It wasn't on the first tier. She climbed on the step stool kept for reaching the higher levels and continued looking. Rims of wheels, several heavy stripped bolts, a honeycomb-shaped metal panel that she thought had something to do with the space program. There are a million reasons why it wouldn't be here. She tried to think of them and couldn't. In fact, though, it was here. It was. In a corner of the third tier, almost hidden behind another bin, still in the Fun World plastic bag with Bobo's face printed on it. When she reached in the bag and her hand closed on the cold steel she wanted to shout in jubilation.

She carried the bag to the hardness tester. Before putting the metal on the anvil, she took several breaths to calm herself down. Steadier after a minute, she positioned the steel on the platform, made sure it was level, and brought it into contact with the penetrator. When the pointer was vertical, she adjusted the dial so the zero was exactly behind the pointer.

Footsteps. Fernando, making his rounds. She turned the crank to apply the major load and watched the pointer jump, swing, and come to rest. Now, pull the crank to take the load off and read the dial.

Sixty-five on Rockwell B.

She was filled with unreasoning, uncritical happiness. Sixty-five on Rockwell B. I *was* right.

"Hey, Marina."

She whirled around. Don, several file folders under his arm, stood in the doorway. He was frowning. "What are you doing?" he asked.

Euphoric, she ran to him. "I've just found out what happened to Loopy Doop."

The frown deepened. "Sure. It was vibration because they didn't lubricate it right."

215

"No it wasn't." The words came almost faster than she could talk. "Loopy Doop was made of steel less than half as strong as it should've been. I've just proved it with the hardness test. My God, when you think about it—steel buckets instead of aluminum, and two fat people who rode twice in a row—" She grasped his arm. "I know that's it. I always knew, but the other tests—"

She stopped as she realized. The samples had been switched somehow, and 4140 substituted. With machined samples, chemical samples, you couldn't tell where the steel came from. The only piece you could be sure of was the fracture itself.

Don was looking at her oddly. He moved back a step. So what if he thought she was crazy. This time she knew—*knew*—she had the right explanation.

"I'd better get along. Sandy just sent me back for these." He tapped the files. "See you."

Funny that Sandy had sent Don for something when he'd just told her he and Don had split. She turned back to the hardness tester and repeated the test. Sixty-five on the Rockwell B. All right. Carbon steel, probably, not a high strength heat-treated alloy like 4140. It would've held up all right unless a few things went out of kilter, like an extraheavy load in an extraheavy gondola over the protracted period of two rides.

Somebody had know. Somebody had switched the samples for the tensile test and the chemical analysis. They'd done it even though had it been proved that Fun World got inferior steel from—from whatever the company was, the one in Singapore— If Fun World could prove Singapore had sold them inferior steel they could sue. Who changed the samples? Somebody from Singapore?

216

She put the Loopy Doop leg in its bag and took it to the evidence room. Instead of replacing it where she'd found it, she put it in one of the lower bins, under a half-burned ironing-board cover. She relocked the room and, after thinking for a moment, put the key in her pocket instead of in its hiding place.

On the way to her office, she went over the case feverishly. Fun World used to get aluminum gondolas from Gonzales Manufacturing. Gonzales lost the contract and went broke. Then Fun World bought steel from the place in Singapore, whatever its name was. Steel gondolas, steel parts for the rides, including legs for Loopy Doop.

She had to call Sandy. First, she wanted the printout with the list of suppliers, so she could get the name of the Singapore place. A lot of that stuff was probably still in her filing cabinet. She unlocked it and found the printout in the bottom drawer where she'd tossed it in her rush to leave for India.

She leafed through the printout. Singapore Metal Works. The contact was somebody named K. M. Lee.

Fun World could've sued Singapore Metal. Maybe they couldn't sue Singapore Metal, though. Maybe Fun World knew what they were getting. But why buy inferior steel instead of the best?

She remembered Enrique Gonzales, embittered after the family's factory closed. What had he said? *Money, lady. Don't you know that's what everything's about?*

Money. Buy steel from Singapore, except you don't get what's listed on the invoices, but something only a third as strong and less than half as expensive, that you figure is still good enough to do the job. What's the cost differential? A lot, if you buy a lot of steel. So you pay for the good stuff, get the bad stuff, and you and Singapore divide the difference fifty-fifty, and everything's fine until you kill a couple of people and maim a few more, and then you have to scramble like crazy.

She had to tell Sandy. She dialed his number, and the line was busy. She hung up and thought: Suppose Sandy knew. Maybe he switched the samples himself. She moved her hand away from the telephone.

Trying to decide what to do, she riffled back through the printout. Something caught her eye. What had it been? She turned a few pages, searching. Another page. There it was. The Delightful Novelty Company of Bombay, India. Contact: V. Shah.

Marina stared at the line of print. It said that the Delightful Novelty Company supplied Fun World with prizes for the games arcade. Brightly painted wooden toys, maybe. Plastic whirligigs on the ends of sticks.

After a moment of suspension, it broke over her. I was testing the steel, talking about how it might not be strong enough. Don't do anything as stupid and crude as try to intimidate me. Let me intimidate myself, take myself off the case, get myself out of the way to leave more room to maneuver—more time to fix up maintenance records that look like they've been faked. More time to melt down Loopy Doop.

Someone broke into Clara's and looked at my file. Cloud Sister, Rain Sister, Nagarajan, the Hotel Rama. Someone asked questions about Patrick. Someone trumped up letters and got Vincent Shah to send them, got him to make a phone call. It didn't take that much. I jumped at it.

She was first aware of her anger as a metallic taste. It spread to fill her head, her hands, her body. She stood up.

218

I'll tell the police. I'll shout it on street corners if I have to.

The Loopy Doop fracture. That was the proof. She hurried out of her office and across the pier toward the testing section, digging in her jacket pocket for the evidence-room key.

The sound of Fernando's chair scraping made her look toward the front door. Someone was coming in. Instinctively, she ran the last few steps to the testing section and hid in the doorway. Across the pier, she saw Don come in the front door and speak to Fernando at his table. Don, who could've switched the samples as easily as Sandy could. And I was telling him all about my great discovery.

As Don and Fernando talked, Fernando waved his arm in her direction, and she pressed closer to the wall. After a few more minutes' conversation, Fernando stood up and went outside.

She waited. Don stood by Fernando's table, shifting his weight in a jittery little dance. After a few minutes, the front door opened again. It wasn't Fernando. Tall, blond, wearing a dark overcoat, Jack Sondergard walked in and looked around him.


They know I'm still here. That's what Don asked Fernando. They've told Fernando something, done something to him to get him out of the way. He wouldn't be suspicious of anything Don said. Don and Sondergard were talking. Sondergard touched Don's cheek, and she could almost feel the light touch of his fingertips on her own face. Don shook his head, and Sondergard put his arms around him, and Marina saw Don's curly hair bright against the shoulder of Sondergard's overcoat.

So Jack went to bed with me, sent me off to India, all in the interest of saving his ass. She remembered clinging to him, overwhelmed with need. He had understood her need perfectly, as he must understand Don's. He had to understand, to be able to use them so well. Who understands Jack's needs, though? Possibly K. M. Lee, at Singapore Metal Works.

Sondergard released Don and started toward her, leaving Don behind him at the door. Marina moved back into the testing section, feeling her way around the machinery to the door of the evidence room. The key was slippery from the sweat of her hand, and the room was dark, but she managed to fit it into the lock and get through the door as she heard Sondergard's footsteps approaching.

Moments after the door closed behind her, a bright outline appeared around its edge. He'd switched on the light. She heard him move to the desk where the key was usually kept and stop.

He was here to get Loopy Doop too, not just to look for her. While she was gone, it hadn't been worth the risk of arousing suspicion by destroying the fractured steel itself, but now he'd have to. Evidence did sometimes get lost, and of course they'd still have imprints and photos of the break. Nobody could check hardness from an imprint or a photo. Since maintenance was set to take the rap, there probably wouldn't be a trial anyway. Fun World would try to settle out of court.

All was quiet. He'd be feeling around for the key, opening the little box— She heard his feet shuffle, then the sound of his steps quickly receding.

As long as Don was at the door she could never get across the open expanse of the pier's interior without being seen. She was stuck. She moved to the bin where she'd hidden Loopy Doop under the ironing-board cover.

Jack Sondergard. Had Bobo been in on it too? Maybe not. Bobo had put her on the case, as the maintenance chief had called Breakdown in, without Jack's OK. The minute that happened Jack started to poke around for something to use against me if he needed to. He struck a gold mine. If I weren't in such bad trouble I'd have to laugh. What a bonanza he got.

She heard steps coming back. What now? Kick the door in, shoot the lock off like in the movies? There was nowhere to hide. She stood with her back to the bin where Loopy Doop was and locked her knees, standing as straight as she could.

No shots, no battering force. Simply the sound of the key slipping into the lock and turning, then the blinding light pouring into the evidence room and Sondergard's silhouette in the doorway. Don had a master key. Too bad she hadn't thought about that.

"So here you are," Sondergard said.

"Right back where I started from."

He moved into the room and now she could see him better. The lines in his face, the circles under his eyes, were deeper than ever.

"You really screwed up with Loopy Doop, Jack," she said.

"You're telling me." He moved toward her. "Where's the sample?"

"You expect me to give it to you?"

"Why not?" He sounded tired. "Really, Marina. When you come down to it, what the hell is it to you?"

"Why should I let you get away with murder?"

"It wasn't murder. It was a miscalculation." He took another step.

"You made me think Catherine might be alive, sent me screaming to India—"

"That was the only part of the whole thing that was interesting. I even read a little of the Rig Veda. I don't apologize. The trip probably did you a world of good."

"Is what you're going through worth the money you got from Singapore Metal Works?"

"I haven't run the calculation lately." He was close now. She might have smelled lime, but maybe it was her imagination. "I need the sample."

"You can't have it."

"You don't think I've gone through this shit to let you put the brakes on, do you?"

No. I think you get the sample, and I—go into the bay, maybe. Depressed over recent traumas in India.

She moved away slightly and said, "You want the sample?"

"I said—"

"Take it." She pulled the plastic Fun World bag out of the bin and swung it at him. The steel caught him in the ribs and he bent over, his face contorted. He fell heavily to his knees.

As she backed away, she heard Don's voice saying, tentatively, "Jack?"

He was in the doorway. She got ready to swing again, but he rushed past her to kneel at Sondergard's side.

Clutching the bag, she ran for the door.

Several weeks later, Marina received a letter from Vijay:

*My dear Marina,*

*What an incredible business this is, indeed! I have spoken with Mr. Vincent Shah, and he admits to sending the letters and making the telephone call, but he says Mr. Sondergard told him it was for a joke on a friend only. He is very frightened, and will cooperate with the police to the fullest extent.*

*It seems you hardly need Mr. Shah to bring Mr. Sondergard to justice. Imagine a man who would put the lives of others, children even, in danger for his own gain! And trick you into coming to India, too! Although for that I think, evil as he is, I owe him a debt.*

*There are now few newspaper stories about Nagarajan-Baladeva. I have heard, though, that the people around Goti are saying he is not dead at all, and will return in another guise. People always wish to believe such things, I think.*

*Sushila and I are to be married in a month's time. I shall wear a red turban, and ride a horse, and my young cousin will hold a parasol over my head. It surprises me that my mother did not insist on hiring an elephant for the occasion!*

*I will close this letter now, Marina. I think of you often.*

*Vijay*

Marina put the letter down on the kitchen table, amid the clutter of a late Saturday breakfast. She would write soon and tell Vijay how the case against Sondergard was progressing. The Fun World empire was in turmoil, was probably finished. Bobo, energized more by fury at Sondergard, she thought, than anything else, was running the company. "The crap he used to tell me about you you wouldn't believe," he had said when she visited him. "He even told me—you have to forgive me for saying this—he even told me you'd made some sort of advances to him. Can you beat that?" His eyes reddened with indignation.

"He had to control, to manipulate everything," she had said to Sandy, realizing she was talking as much about Nagarajan as Sondergard. Sandy was gray, shaken. Don's defection had devastated him. He spent a lot of time talking about security measures, procedures to assure he would never be betrayed again. "He didn't realize complete control isn't possible," she said.

"I'm damn well going to have complete control of this place from now on," Sandy said.

Balmy air drifted through the open window, and sunlight gleamed on leftover jam, toast crumbs, the last half-cup of coffee. In another apartment, somebody's stereo was playing. She listened. The music was faint, but it might have been the Vivaldi that was one of Patrick's favorites. Impossible to tell for sure. When it ended, she got up. She had decided to make a phone call.

# About the Author

Mickey Friedman is a former reporter and book reviewer for the *San Francisco Examiner*. She is now living in New York and has recently completed her third novel.

# Attention Mystery and Suspense Fans

Do you want to complete your collection of mystery and suspense stories by some of your favorite authors? Raymond Chandler, Erle Stanley Gardner, Ed McBain, Cornell Woolrich, among many others, and included in Ballantine's new Mystery Brochure.

For your FREE Mystery Brochure, fill in the coupon below and mail it to:

# MURDER...
# MAYHEM...
# MYSTERY...

## From Ballantine

TA-43